DEATH BY PIRATES

PATRICIA FISHER: SHIP'S DETECTIVE BOOK 3

STEVE HIGGS

Publisher: Steve Higgs

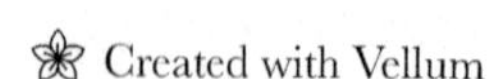
Created with Vellum

To Debbie Arnold. Thank you for reading.

PROLOGUE

THE ANGELICA PARADOX

"The snake is essentially defanged," I quipped. "Angelica has lost all her power now that we know it is her behind all the recent shenanigans."

Barbie didn't see it the same way as me. "But she's still free to organise another attack, Patty. What will she do next? She could still be on the ship."

I agreed. "She probably is."

Angelica Howard-Box was proving far harder to locate than I had ever imagined. The Aurelia, the giant cruise ship on which Barbie and I both work and live, is basically a small town with the streets stacked one atop the other twenty times. You might think that finding a single person ought to not be all that hard, but trust me we had been going at the job for several days and had nothing to show for our efforts.

If you are wondering what I am wittering on about, my name is Patricia Fisher. I come from a small village in the southeast corner of England and through a confluence of circumstances now find myself employed as the detective on board the world's finest luxury cruise liner.

My life, in general, is blissfully wonderful.

Barbie lives with me in the Windsor Suite, the finest suite on the entire ship which comes with a price tag I cannot possibly hope to afford. My accommodation, along with a huge manor house in England, cars, money, and other things all come to me courtesy of the Maharaja of Zangrabar. I found something that belonged to him a while back and then saved his life and his throne.

He insists that he and his entire country are in my debt. It weighs on me sometimes.

I met Barbie the day I came aboard the ship. I was a passenger at the time and running from a situation I didn't wish to face, but that's a story for another time. I also met my butler, Jermaine, and a host of other people who have become my friends.

It's less than a half a year since I first set eyes on the Aurelia, yet it feels like a lifetime, and I can barely remember who I was before this part of my life started.

The only shadow hanging over me is the one cast by Angelica. We grew up together and she hated me even when we were kids. One might expect that such a strong emotion would wane over time, yet hers has continued to grow in its intensity.

Okay, so I had provoked her a teensy bit, and every time she tried to do anything to get one over on me, I made sure it massively backfired. Oh, and then there was her son's wedding which I sort of ruined. Though, to be fair, all I did was make the bride and groom admit how they really felt. Angelica didn't care that they were not in love. She just wanted her millionaire footballer son to marry the gorgeous internet sensation superstar so they could make a huge pile of money and become the new Beckhams.

The wedding ceremony never took place and … well, I guess she was kinda sore about it still because she was on the Aurelia somewhere and doing her best to wreck my life. So far, she had tried to cause a rift between me and Barbie, tried to get me sacked, tried to break up my romance with the captain, and had broken into my suite, zapping Jermaine with a stun gun as she did, to then trash all my clothes and steal my jewellery.

That she had failed in all but the last of those was more luck than anything else, but having recently solved a case involving snakes and drugs and a love triangle gone wrong, I had finally been able to focus my efforts on figuring out where she was.

However, as I already said, our efforts were yet to produce a result.

There were posters displayed around the ship asking passengers 'Have you seen this woman?'. Angelica was here somewhere, and the security team employed on board were being extra vigilant with the passengers leaving and returning to the ship. I was confident she could not get off, but I also believed she had help.

To start with there was the stun gun that was used on Jermaine. I would not claim sneaking a weapon on board is impossible, but it is difficult. I thought it more likely she had a member or members of the crew in her employ. One of them, especially if they were part of the ship's security detail, could have supplied the stun gun.

Then there was the computer hacking which was far beyond Angelica. Someone with skills, according to my friends who knew about such things, had hacked my computer, created a clone email account, and proceeded to copy my files. Some sensitive ones had been leaked to the press, causing embarrassment to the cruise line and the captain.

Angelica also found the captain's former fiancé and convinced her to play a part in ruining our relationship. She came so close to succeeding, I refused to think about it.

I needed to find Angelica and have her ejected from the ship. However, she was wilier than I would have given her credit for, so after extensive cabin-to-cabin searching and painstakingly reviewing the passenger manifest several times, we were yet to find her.

She wasn't listed as a passenger and her face had not been recorded by the ship's central registry system. It further proved there had to be crewmembers working with her.

So what could I do? Well, the answer to that, in my opinion, was to defang the snake. It wasn't the best analogy because it meant I was the mouse. Sticking with it though, the mouse was defeating the snake by moving out of striking range: we were leaving the ship.

We had just docked at the town of Torruga on the western coast of the British Union Isles. A tiny spot of land rising from the

Atlantic Ocean, I had never been here before and it was not a place the Aurelia often stopped because the port could only accommodate one cruise ship at a time.

Me and all my friends were going to disarm Angelica by spending tonight and the next day exploring the island. We had even booked a horseback excursion to the famous Haden Falls, a natural landmark of outstanding beauty. It was a great plan. It was my plan. It was going to give us some respite from her attacks while I figured out how we were going to beat her.

Yeah. I'm stupid.

1

THE UNEXPECTED CLIENT

The moon carved a path above our heads as we stepped out from underneath the awning that covered the royal suites' exit. The British Union Isles in the middle of the Atlantic is one of those odd little places that people just never get to visit. The island doesn't have any roads which makes it unlike anywhere else on earth.

There are no cars, obviously, just horses/ponies, bicycles, and rickshaws made with bicycles. It also isn't big enough for a proper airport, so only small craft can get to it, but sitting so far from any other piece of land, small aircraft must be specially adapted to make the journey.

Consequently, the only planes coming in and out are those carrying essential supplies. Everything else arrives by boat. The island has one deep water port and a good thing too for cruise ship tourists account for thirty percent of the island's GDP according to Alistair.

That's my boyfriend, in case you didn't know. Alistair Huntley is the captain of the cruise ship, and he is offensively handsome. Quite why he continues to lavish me with his affections I cannot fathom, but he claims to love me and backs his words up with actions.

I am a very lucky lady, and I was feeling it today.

Today was one of those amazing days when I had no cases to investigate. Well, there were cases, I was just choosing not to investigate them. One was little more than a rumour – a discrepancy with the onboard casino takings. Something wasn't tallying, but no robbery had taken place and I was yet to be officially task with investigating it.

There was always something to investigate if I chose to, but I was overdue some time off, so my friends and I were leaving the ship to spend the next day exploring an incredible paradise island and I didn't have a care in the world.

Okay, so that's not exactly true, but if I ignore the Angelica Howard-Box situation, there is very little troubling my mind. We would return to the ship late tonight and leave again early in the morning, minimising the time during which Angelica could do anything.

My dachshunds, two little ladies called Anna and Georgie, were snoozing in my suite though more normally I would take them with me. It was busy in the small coastal town – a festival was in full swing; the music and hubbub of conversation audible even from the ship. My little sausage dogs would fret if I took them out into the crowds, and I knew I would end up carrying them to ensure they didn't get trodden on.

Won't Angelica go after them? Good question - I already admitted she broke into my suite once before. To combat that very chance, I had enlisted the help of a friendly member of the security team. Lieutenant Kashmir had volunteered, in fact, leaping at the chance to dog sit my snuggly babies while lavishing himself in the luxury of my suite for the next twenty-four hours.

He was on duty, so far as Alistair was concerned, and would be armed and ready should Angelica come calling.

Breaking my train of thought before it could turn dark, my blonde friend, Barbie, grabbed my arm.

"Oh, my goodness!" she squeaked in a high-pitched and excited tone. "Look at all the people in costume!"

Now that we were on the quayside, the vague ant-like shapes we could see from the top deck had become people and Barbie was right – everywhere a person chose to look, they were dressed up to look like pirates. That's no exaggeration, literally everyone in view was dressed as a pirate and it was clearly something the islanders put some effort into because these were not costumes bought over the internet, they were handmade and authentic looking.

The British Union Isles has a troubled history – I vaguely remember reading something about it in school many years ago. So far from its sovereign nation, Great Britain, the small island found itself to be a pirate haven. Trader ships would stop off on their way across the ocean and that made their routes predictable and thus targetable.

A British garrison had been wiped out during a battle if I recalled my history correctly.

"Wow," gasped Molly. "This is going to be great. I love pirates."

"Me too," trumpeted my assistant, Sam.

The sudden whizz of fireworks shooting skywards drew my eyes in time to see them explode high above our heads. People cheered and it was hard to resist relaxing into the island's party mood. I didn't even try. Ahead there were people carrying large plastic margarita cups and wearing gaudy Mardi Gras style beads and headpieces.

It was a heady place to be.

Following me out as we left the ship behind and started toward the town were Barbie, Jermaine, Sam, Molly, Deepa, Martin, and Sam's gran, Gloria. Alistair had tasks to complete, but planned to join us later. Molly, Deepa, and Martin are all members of the ship's security team. Deepa and Martin are assigned to work with me as I try to keep crime to a minimum and solve the cases that do occur. Molly arrived as a new member of the security team just a few days ago. She isn't assigned to me, but used to be my housemaid in England and feels at home with the people she knows. Sam is someone I took on as my assistant when I set myself up as a private investigator in England a while back. His granny is along for the trip because Sam has Downs and needs someone to be around to pick up after him.

Barbie is a best friend I met the day I came on board. She's a gym instructor and has the kind of body most women can only dream about. That just leaves Jermaine. He is my rock. He is the man I love more than any other in the world, probably including Alistair, but it is a platonic love ensured by differing sexual preferences and a few decades age gap. He is also my butler, a position he need not maintain, but one he insists is his deepest pleasure.

If anything were to ever happen to him … I shudder to imagine what I might become.

"Whew, it is hot here," Lieutenant Commander Martin Baker took out a handkerchief to dab at his neck and forehead.

Nobody argued or felt a need to comment – he wasn't wrong, but the heat was glorious, and it was only going to get hotter when the sun rose in the morning.

Barbie, leading our gaggle as she headed for the barrier rope keeping the crowds back, turned around to walk backwards. Clapping her hands together gleefully, she asked, "What shall we do first? Is anyone hungry? Or shall we get on with exploring?"

"Mrs Fisher?" the raised voice cut off any answer Barbie might have got and caused seven sets of eyeballs to swing to our left. It became eight sets when Barbie swung back around to see where the call had come from. "Mrs Fisher. Patricia Fisher." A hand rose in the crowd.

The quayside was lined with hundreds of people who were mostly there to sell tourist rubbish to the cruise ship guests. 'Get to them first' seemed to be the unspoken motto for we met the same crowd everywhere we went, only the people and the things they held ever changed.

I squinted into the press of people as I tried to make out who had called my name and just as I did, the person whose hand was held high in the air stepped between the people blocking my view.

I'm not sure why, but I expected to see someone I knew. However, the identity of the man now lowering his hand was a mystery. He was white and in his early sixties. A white cotton shirt, the style with no collar and buttons going to the navel but not beyond, sat above trim cotton shorts and a pair of newish brown deck shoes. On his head was a straw boater hat that would have looked at home on board a punt going down the River Thames at Henley in the summer.

I mentally labelled his style as island chic, but though he had my eye now, I genuinely didn't wish to talk to him. Whatever it was that he wanted, it was almost certainly something I could do without – something important to him, but not to me, in all likelihood.

However, I am not one for rudeness, and had already made eye contact. To walk away without speaking to him would be a terrible display of manners, so with a sigh that I kept inside my body, I smiled and altered my trajectory.

"Who is that, Patty?" asked Barbie, her eyebrows wiggling as she tried to figure out if she should know who it was.

From the side of my mouth I said, "I have no idea."

The man's hands were on the barrier rope now, a device that kept the crowds back by implying they ought to remain on the other side rather than by creating an impenetrable wall. He was waiting for me to get closer and when I did, he extended his right hand for me to shake.

"Mrs Fisher, I apologise for stopping you. My name is Edward Teach and I am in need of your skills."

My brain was about to kick my mouth into gear, my plan to explain that I was here on holiday cut off when he carried on talking.

"I am willing to pay you and your team a million dollars US for their help."

My mouth stopped moving and I could tell without looking that his wild statement had caught the attention of all my friends. They were all around me and suddenly giving Mr Teach their full attention.

"I'm in," said Molly. "Where do I sign up? Is there a cash bonus for being first to volunteer?"

"Me too," echoed Gloria. "My pension doesn't pay diddly."

I lifted my arms to either side, begging for calm.

"Hold on, everyone. Hold on." When they settled down, which took a few seconds because Molly was already figuring out how to spend her share and asking if it would be an even split, I fixed Edward Teach with a challenging expression. "What is it that you want us to do, Mr Teach and why would you be willing to part with a million dollars just like that."

Edward nodded his head, turning to the side and taking a pace. Immediately, I noticed a heavy limp and the look of discomfort behind his eyes. I wondered if it might be connected to whatever he wanted to hire me for. Before I could ask him, he started to speak.

"To answer the second part of your question first, I am exceedingly rich."

"Are you also single?" asked Molly. I was fairly certain she was joking – there had to be forty years between them though I'd seen couples with greater age gaps. One pair I'd met on board were lining up to get married right now, in fact.

Edward swung his head around to stare at Molly with his eyebrows raised for a second before choosing to bring his gaze back to me without replying to her.

Picking up where he left off, he said, "A million dollars is not a big deal to me, not when I fear my life might be in jeopardy. That, of course, answers the first part of your question – I want you to keep me alive."

His request triggered a warning buzzer in my head. Okay I'm a detective by profession and I'll not deny there was an instant tug of interest, but I was here for what could easily be the only visit I would ever get – the Aurelia did not routinely stop at the British Union Isles. I wanted to savour it, to explore and sample the wonderfully diverse culture. Becoming embroiled in an investigation was not on my list of things to do.

"I'm sorry, Mr Teach," I replied without really needing to think. "I am only here for a little more than twenty-four hours, and my intention is to relax and enjoy myself. I must decline your offer."

I made to move away but my friends were bunched in around me and they were talking in excited, animated terms.

"I volunteer myself," said Molly.

"Me too. I can't wait to get stuck in," agreed Gloria.

"And me!" trumpeted Sam with glee.

I had turned away from the eccentric rich person, but that just meant I could see the hope in the faces around me.

"My wife and I are part of the ship's security detail," announced Martin. "Deepa and I will protect you while we are here."

It was the money. I could tell that was the factor motivating my friends and I understood why they felt driven to change their plans. There were eight of us and that made for a significant pay out for what might be a small amount of effort. From Martin's perspective, he and Deepa could earn enough to buy a house.

No one was saying it, but they all wanted me to agree to be part of the team.

"I'm only interested if Mrs Fisher is involved," stated Edward Teach without a modicum of hesitation and in so doing he sealed my fate.

Barbie gave me an apologetic smile. "It is a lot of money, Patty." What she didn't say was that of all the people in our group, I was the only one who didn't need it.

When I uncovered the Maharaja's sapphire all those months ago, I received a pay out from the insurance firm who originally underwrote it. I shared it with Barbie and Jermaine at the time and believe me they earned every penny. It was a handsome amount, but divided by three, it made a pleasing nest egg for my two friends and no more than that.

Unable to fight the inevitable, I twisted back around to face the hopeful client.

"What exactly is it that you want us to do, Edward?"

2

GHOST STORY

We had been off the ship for ten minutes and all my plans had already gone out of the window. Edward's house, he explained, was set high above the harbour at the edge of a cliff. It was a mercy he had a team of rickshaw taxi chaps waiting to take us to it because I did not fancy walking it.

The rickshaws were limited to two people -otherwise the poor chaps pedalling them up the winding cliff path might never have got there. I settled in next to Edward and listened to his tale though I asked him for the bullet point version, intending to have him explain more fully when all the team was able to listen.

"The story I have to tell you will sound bizarre, Mrs Fisher," he began to explain why he felt a need to hire my services. "It started two hundred years ago. My family line can be traced back to a pirate of some repute, Mrs Fisher." He paused from speaking to twist in his seat and make sure he had eye contact. "You may have heard the name 'Blackbeard'?"

I found my eyebrows knitting together, unsure where his explanation was going. I nodded though.

"Of course." I knew his name, but now that I thought about it, my memory served up a pertinent snippet of detail. "His real name was Edward Teach, wasn't it?"

Was I being conned? Was this an elaborate trick being played by my friends?

"Indeed, Mrs Fisher."

"Call me Patricia, please," I begged – I already had far too many people in my life who insisted on addressing me formally.

With a nod of acknowledgement, he continued, "As I said, my family has a troubled past. The original Edward Teach died in battle in 1718, but not without leaving behind a son who followed his father's notorious footsteps. Many of my male ancestors met with unfortunate ends, but the most famous in these parts is my great, great, great, great, great, great grandfather who also engaged in acts of piracy. Do you know much of this island's history?"

I shook my head. What little I believed I knew could easily be wrong.

"I won't go into great depth, Patricia, but suffice to say that the British Union Isles acted as a stop off point for ships sailing to the new world and as such was a magnet for piracy. A little more than two centuries ago, the king of England, King George, appointed a man called Francis Beaumont to be governor here. His first task was to rid the waters of the pirate scourge."

"And he succeeded?" I found that I had been drawn into Edward's tale.

"Yes, but he took an unexpected route to achieve his aim. He chose to go into business with my ancestor."

My eyebrows rose as I showed my lack of understanding.

"At the time in question, my ancestor, Reginald Teach, was a rich man. He had men at his disposal and a loyal following among the people of the isles because he provided them with food and other goods, sometimes even a share of the stolen booty so the history books say. In exchange, they were prepared to lie and even kill to protect him which meant catching him anywhere other than at sea was an unlikely proposition. At sea he had six heavily armed ships at his disposal. Only a coordinated and well-structured attack was going to defeat him and would come with heavy losses for the winning side. Francis Beaumont offered him a deal in secret, befriending several of the 'women of the town'," he made it clear by his tone he was referring to prostitutes, "to carry the message. Reginald Teach accepted a full pardon from King George in return for handing over every member of his crew. In total one thousand and forty-two men and women were hanged in a public spectacle that lasted three days. His ships were sold off and Reginald accepted a large estate which I now own."

It was an incredible story, not least because I had never heard it before. I was telling myself this was the sort of thing that ought to jump off the page of a history book.

To hurry things along, I said, "Ok, Edward, that's the history. What does that have to do with your current situation?"

Edward Teach looked right into my eyes and reached forward to take my right hand.

"Patricia, you will find this hard to accept, but I believe I am being targeted by the ghosts of the men Reginald Teach betrayed."

Now I don't want to state that his voice had taken on a spooky edge – it was probably just a combination of the darkness pressing in around me and the nature of his words, but I could feel my sense of unease rising. The hairs on the back of my neck were rising and I found myself remembering a case involving a supposed ghost in a bookshop I investigated a few months ago.

"Exactly one hundred years ago today, the descendants of Francis Beaumont were all killed. The entire family line was wiped out in one evening. The sole survivor of the attack was a housemaid who claimed the assailants were pirates risen from their graves, the nooses they were hanged with still trailing from their necks. There was an attack at my house too. It is chronicled in my great, great, great, great grandfather's journal. Two of my family were killed that night but the rest were able to escape, fleeing via a set of old smugglers' tunnels and able to hide out until dawn."

I drew in a deep breath, thinking about all I had just heard before asking, "What makes you think you might be targeted now?"

"By ghosts you mean? I do not believe in ghosts, Patricia," he replied with a wry smile. "I apologise for the theatrics, but I needed to explain the background."

I sagged a little in my seat. He had been creeping me out, making me think this was going to be a super spooky investigation that might have us poking around in graveyards or something. Now that he revealed the truth, I got that someone-walking-over-your-grave sensation that sent a spasm of shivers down my spine. It came as a relief that he wasn't going to ask me to investigate an ancient ghost story, but also as a disappointment too because I was beginning to think all we needed to do for the million-dollar prize was keep the raving nutter safe from his own imagination.

Of course, his revelation led me to another rather important question.

"So who is it that you need to be protected from, Edward? I'm an investigator, not a bodyguard."

"That, Patricia, is what I need you to find out. There have been spooky things happening around my house. The story of my family and the great pirate betrayal is no secret – everyone here knows it and they celebrate the story."

Clues aligned in my head. "That's what tonight's pirate festival is about!" I gasped.

Edward nodded. "It's a three-day party to represent the three days over which the pirates were hanged. It happens every year and every year I hide in my house for as much as I can because there are many poor families on the island who still hold a grudge against me for being rich. Rich from the gains my ancestor made by betraying their ancestral family members."

"That's ridiculous," I remarked, struggling to believe anyone would still care two hundred years later. Then I wondered if I was reacting too swiftly. Edward Teach lived in a huge house and had a family fortune. For a person struggling to get by to see it every day and have it serve as a reminder of where the money came from …

"Perhaps so," Edward conceded, "but hiring staff to work in my house has always been a struggle and now I have none. The most recent housemaid I took on vanished last week. I don't mean vanished, vanished." He attempted to clarify. "What I mean is she stopped coming to work. There's more though. I have had threats – notes shoved under my door. Someone is planning to hurt me or worse, Patricia, and I believe they mean to use the legend of my family history as a cover for their crime."

"Do you have any idea who?" I asked. It was the next most obvious question, but the rickshaw chap cycling away in front of us, grunting, groaning, and sweating from his efforts, rounded a corner and what I assumed to be Edward's house came into view.

It was a huge, white colonial building set over two stories. Four tall pillars dominated the front façade sitting two either side of the large front door. Edward had not lied about his house or that he was rich.

The next thing I noticed was how close to the cliff it sat. I could see through the grounds surrounding the house and the land just seemed to end a few yards beyond the building. How far the land extended I could not tell in the darkness, but the backdrop was one of stars like pinpricks of light shining through a black blanket.

Could I sleep in a house like that? I doubted it. I would lie awake every night expecting the cliff to crumble into the sea.

Whether Edward fell silent and omitted to answer my question because we were now so close to his home, or because the rickshaw driver might overhear what could be sensitive information I could not tell. I didn't fight it though, electing to stay quiet as well. For now.

The rickshaw slowed, the driver coasting to a stop near the front steps of Edward's house. In the lead all the way, I could hear the other rickshaws arriving behind me. My friends were remarking about the house and the view.

"Cor!" remarked Molly. "That's even bigger than your place, Mrs Fisher."

Edward paid the rickshaw men individually, I guessed that each worked for themselves and owned their own rickshaw rather than for a firm. When they turned their bicycles around and started back down the hill, Edward indicated toward his house.

"Come along inside, please, everyone. I'm sure you all deserve a drink for volunteering to miss out on tonight's festivities."

In a long line, we all followed the eccentric islander into his home, each of us marvelling at the splendour and luxury we found within. Everything was marble and there were large oil paintings and ancient looking tapestries on the walls.

It was cool inside – a welcome relief from the humidity we had endured since leaving the ship, and true to his word, Edward willingly played the host.

While he did so, he regaled my friends with the same story he'd told me.

When he got to the part about ghosts, Gloria got to her feet.

"That's all for me. I quite fancy making a pile of money, but I'm not messing with evil spirits at my age."

"They aren't real," I assured her.

"Ha! That's what you think. I've seen 'Ghost Detectives' on TV. Every episode they are in another haunted house."

Martin tutted. "Those daft reality shows are all rubbish, Gloria. They all get canned after a series."

Gloria wasn't about to have her mind changed. "That's because they all get sucked into hell!" she cackled.

"Well, I hope they are real," said Sam, grinning. "I like pirates."

"Yeah," agreed Molly, pulling a mean face. "If I see a ghost, I'm just gonna kick it in the nuts."

I had no response to that statement.

Edward spoke again, settling the discussion. "I do not believe they are real, but that just makes them more dangerous."

"How so?" asked Jermaine.

Edward explained his concerns about someone using the old ghost story as a cover and how it was that he had many persons on the island who might wish him harm.

"I have my fingers in many pies," he admitted. "Very little of it is of my own doing, you understand. I inherited everything from my father six years ago when he passed and as I have just explained, my family history is such that we are influential on this island. For two hundred years, very little has happened here without my family's involvement and often with my family's money behind it. This was a good thing, but now I fear it may be my undoing."

"What do you mean?" asked Martin.

"Criminal elements have infiltrated the island. I believe we have become a staging post for drug distribution and other organised crimes. One local criminal in particular has taken an interest in me."

Barbie voiced her confusion, "Surely there is a police force on the island charged with combatting such criminals. Isn't it their job to protect you if you are in danger?"

Edward turned to answer her. "Yes. In theory. However, I believe there may be corrupt elements within the police. It is hard to know who I can trust."

A noise interrupted whatever he was planning to say next, a howl of wind that had not been there before and could only have been made by a door to the outside being opened.

Everyone in the room froze.

3

ATTACK IN THE DARK

Edward's eyes were wide with fear, and I worried mine might be doing the same.

The moment of petrification lasted only for a split second, the braver souls in my group reacting in a manner that came as no surprise to me.

Martin and Deepa immediately turned toward the noise, Jermaine too, which triggered Barbie, Sam, and Molly to react in a similar fashion.

"Edward," I hissed, "are you expecting anyone? Does anyone else live here?"

Looking gravely concerned, he said, "No, I live alone. No one ever comes here."

"Do you have a safe room, Sir?" asked Jermaine. He was without a suit for once, choosing a smart navy polo shirt and a pair of fitted tan shorts which exposed the muscle on his arms and legs. I knew how capable he was with just his hands and feet – the man was like a tall, Jamaican ninja, but if someone was after Edward, and it wasn't just his paranoia, would they come bearing guns?

None of the ship's security officers were armed, their weapons left on board the Aurelia because they had zero jurisdiction once they were outside the dock.

Edward gritted his teeth. "No. No safe room."

"I'm not so sure about this investigation any more," said Molly. "Perhaps we should leave it to …"

A door slammed, the sound cutting her off.

"Leaving is the safest option," announced Martin, taking charge. This was a security operation, not an investigation, and I was happy that no one was looking to me to lead.

With fast strides people began to move, heading for the door to lead out of Edward's kitchen.

"Ooh I hope it's ghost pirates?" gasped Sam excitedly.

Then the lights went out and I wasn't the only one who screamed in shock. The suddenness of it gripped deep in my core, fuelling the fear I already felt. We were hurrying into a hallway that ran through his house, but robbed of our sight, we screeched to a halt, all colliding with each other as we bunched up.

In the darkness of Edward's house, beams of moonlight came through the windows to illuminate patches of the marble floor. My eyes were adjusting to the dark while Edward was being consulted about the quickest way to get out of his house - the general consensus was that we would be safer elsewhere.

However, before we could get moving, the appearance of a dim glow through a door to our front caught everyone's attention.

"Someone's coming," remarked Deepa unnecessarily. There was grit to her words, and it came as no surprise when she set off to intercept whoever was there. Martin went with her. Molly close behind.

Sam went to follow, but I grabbed his arm and held him back, whispering, "Keep me safe, Sam," so he would believe he was looking after me, not being kept close by my side because I was worried about him.

Deepa, Molly, and Martin vanished around a corner, leaving the rest of us in a huddle. I had Jermaine with me and under any other circumstances that would make me feel quite safe. Tonight was a different case, accentuated the very next moment when someone who wasn't part of our group chose to speak.

"Edward Teach ..." an eerie voice drifted through the silent house. "You must pay for the crimes of your forefathers. Come forth and settle your debt."

To say the voice gave me the heebie geebies would be a massive understatement. I wasn't far from wetting myself, and then I saw something that would stay with me for the rest of my life.

Appearing in the light coming through a window, a figure stepped into the hallway to our left. That the person I was looking at was dead and had been for a very long time never even got questioned as the detail of the face, clothes, and features slammed into my brain.

The moonlight caught on its right arm, revealing the radius and ulnar bones. A rag of cloth from what was once the pirate's shirt hung limply beneath his elbow, but my attention was drawn rather sharply to the object in his hand.

When the pirate lifted his arm, the sharp edge of a cutlass flashed when it passed through the light of the moon.

Gloria swore and she was not the only one.

Jermaine immediately swung toward the dead pirate, facing the danger head on when the rest of us were thinking that running away was a much better idea.

"Jermaine, sweetie," I stammered, reaching out to grab his arm and consequently letting go of Sam's.

"I'm getting out of here!" blurted Edward, the terror in his voice palpable. "The ghosts are real! It's all real!" Panicked, he started running, heading away from the apparition now blocking the hallway.

I shouted, "Edward, no! Stay together!"

Jermaine twitched with indecision and when a shout of pain from Martin then echoed from somewhere deep in the house it only added to the confusion.

Sam yelled, "I'll get Edward!" and ran after him.

I shouted for Sam to stop. I knew the ghosts were not real – they couldn't be – but that was little comfort because it made them no less dangerous.

Barbie slapped my shoulder as she set off, "I'll get them," she announced, splitting our team yet again. Sam was already out of sight and Barbie was gone the next moment. It left just me, Jermaine, and Gloria. Nine had been reduced to three in a handful of seconds. If the 'ghosts' wanted to divide us into manageable portions, they had achieved it without even trying.

"Sweetie," I prompted Jermaine again.

The dead pirate wasn't advancing. He blocked the hallway but that wasn't the way we wanted to go – the front door was in the opposite direction where Edward, Sam, and then Barbie had gone.

Jermaine bared his teeth, wanting to attack the apparition and reveal its true nature, but able to acknowledge we were in trouble and if he moved, he would leave me exposed – the one thing he would never do.

With a reluctant nod, he said, "To the front door, please, ladies. I believe it is time we departed this house."

I could hear Deepa, Martin, and Molly. They were shouting loud enough that we would hear them even if we were outside.

As we started toward the door, I shouted, "Deepa! We are leaving! Get out of the house!" We were making our best pace, Gloria moaning about her hip as she hustled down the hallway.

"I told you ghosts are real," she remarked somewhat triumphantly.

Jermaine ran a few yards ahead, checking doorways to make sure no one was about to jump out and ambush us, and we made it to the front door unmolested.

The lobby to Edward's house, a double height showpiece with a sweeping staircase down each side, let in more light than anywhere else. Coming from a dim corridor into the moonlit entrance with caution, we could instantly see that our route to the exit was clear.

Jermain ran ahead again, opening the front door to peer outside.

"There's no one outside," he reported which was both good news and bad. Good because there were no returned-from-the-grave-pirates toting swords and waiting to kill us, but bad because where were Sam, Barbie, and Edward?

We got clear of the house, Jermaine gently and with great care, sweeping Gloria from her feet to run with her in his arms. We kept going, putting a little distance between us and the building, but once we were twenty yards away and in a wide-open space, I stopped. Turning around to face the house, I screamed for the rest of my friends.

"Sam! Barbie! Molly!" I wanted them all to come running out of the house. We were going to head back down the hill and get back on the ship. Poor Edward was going to have to figure this out for himself. I'd dealt with enough dangerous situations in my recent past to know that this one was beyond my calling. He could offer as much money as he wanted, but I wasn't going to get involved and neither were any of my friends.

I heard a shout, but couldn't work out whose voice it was. It could have been any one of the girls.

Sucking in a huge lungful of air, I bellowed their names again, this time listing them all so no one would feel left out or less important to me. With the echo of my voice still fading into the darkness, I stared at the blackened house. A second ticked by, then another.

Jermaine started forward.

"Wait here, madam. I will be as swift as I can."

I didn't want him to go back inside, but I was terrified for my friends. How had our evening of fun gone so bad so quickly?

Just as he got moving, voices came from just inside the door and Deepa emerged. She was moving fast and had an arm around Martin. He had a hand pressed to his left side and was clearly wounded, the dark stain of blood showing on his shirt. Molly had his other side, the two women keeping him moving.

They came down the steps two at a time, Jermaine and me rushing forward to get them. They were out of breath and just as wide-eyed as the rest of us.

I screamed, "Barbie!" through the door and got a reply though it didn't come from inside the house. She appeared a moment later, jogging around the corner of the house to our right. I gasped a sigh of relief that she didn't appear to be hurt, but it ended prematurely when I saw what was missing. "Wait, where's Sam?"

Barbie's footsteps faltered and she squinted at us, then across at Gloria, and then behind her.

"What, he didn't find his way back to you?"

With Martin, Deepa, and Molly in tow, we were moving away from the house again, but I let them carry on because I needed to stop.

"You went after him, Barbie," I wailed. "I thought he was with you. You didn't see him?"

She closed the distance between us, coming close enough that I could see the worry in her eyes.

"No. I was chasing shadows. I almost ran into one of those … things, but backed up and went the other way. I didn't want to shout for Sam; I figured I would catch up to him outside. Eventually, I found a door and that's when I came to see if everyone else got out. Where's Edward?" she asked, looking around again. "Maybe he took Sam the long way around."

I couldn't decide what to do. Sam was missing and I had to resolve that no matter what. I yelled his name, Barbie joining in. Behind us, Deepa, Martin, and the others lent their voices, filling the night with our desperate demands.

No reply came back.

I was breathing heavily, pain clawing at my heart as the borderline panic inside me threatened to burst through the barrier and sweep me away. My head spun.

Gasping at my own stupidity when I realised I could just phone him, I yanked out my mobile and dialled his number. It rang and rang, my frustration and fear climbing with every second. When it went to voicemail, I cut the call off and tried again. I got the same result.

"We have to go back in and look for him," I murmured to myself, staring into the dark hole where the front door still hung open. My brain caught up to me a heartbeat later, jolting me into motion as I remembered Martin.

"How badly is he hurt?" I gushed, running across the grass to see him.

Barbie hadn't noticed that he was wounded. "What happened?" she gasped.

We were going away from the house, joining our friends to regroup, but Gloria had her handbag hitched high on her shoulder and was heading for the house with determination etched on her jaw.

"Gloria where are you going?" I moved to block her path.

She tried to go around me. "I'm going to find my grandson," she growled angrily.

Molly choked, "What about the ghosts?"

"They're not ghosts," I shot back. My remark silenced everyone. Now that they were looking at me, I said, "They can't be. There's no such thing."

Martin hitched an eyebrow. "Well, I don't know too much about that, but whatever cut me vanished through a wall."

"It did," Deepa backed him up. "I was right behind Martin when it happened. We were trying to catch up with it but every time it turned a corner, it seemed to gain ten feet on us. We just couldn't close the distance."

Molly joined in. "And then we went around a corner, and it was there. It slashed at Martin and ran right through a wall."

Gloria tried to go around me again. "That's as may be, but I'm going to look for Sam anyway."

I hated the lack of options I faced, but stopped blocking Gloria so I could turn around and go with her.

"I'm coming with you."

It came as no surprise when Jermaine's deep bass voice boomed out. "I shall accompany you, madam."

Martin wheezed, "Then we are all going. Strength in numbers. There will be weapons in the house – knifes in the kitchen, I think I saw a sword on a wall."

"Sweetie, you are injured," I pointed out.

Martin Baker yanked his shirt back into place where Deepa and Barbie had been examining his wound.

"It's superficial. Besides, there'll be a first aid kit in the house somewhere too, or some sheets we can use for bandages. We need to call the local law enforcement too."

Just minutes after escaping Edward's house of horror and the terrifying spectres we'd seen within, we all went back through the front door.

4

THE SEARCH

No one knew what the number for emergency services was on the British Union Isles, but when a call back to the ship revealed that it was three nines just like in Britain, I almost slapped my palm to my face. Why hadn't I thought to simply try that and see if it connected?

Deepa dealt with the police, talking to the dispatcher while we crept through the house. We were not trying to be quiet and were using the lights on our phones to illuminate wherever we went.

Continuing to call for Sam and Edward yielded no result other than deathly silence, my own paranoia climbing with each passing minute.

It took us ten minutes to find the master power switch. We started in the kitchen where almost everyone armed themselves. I chose to abstain – I don't like knives and would feel more scared carrying one, the fear based on the likelihood that I would accidentally stab one of my own party. Or myself. Gloria picked up a cleaver and was most dismayed when I relieved her of it and put it back in the drawer.

Having exhausted all the places we could think of to look in the house, we moved outside where we found a small brick shack housing a generator. I was constantly jumping at shadows, freaked out by the 'ghosts' and wishing we could get the electricity restored.

Worryingly, the generator was still running, and the power switch was set to the on position. Questioning what was keeping the lights off made my stomach flutter a little. Thankfully, Jermaine solved that mystery when he explored a little further and found a fuse box.

"It's tripped out," he stated, lifting the clear plastic lid, and flicking a switch.

Instantly, a bare lightbulb sprang into life above our heads. It brought some relief but not a lot – we still hadn't found Sam or Edward.

This time the group had stayed together, all seven of us sticking like glue in the dark. With the electricity back on, searching the house would be simpler and my friends were already leaving the brick shack with the generator on their way back there.

I started to follow, but a door with a padlock caught my eye. It was set into the wall farthest from the entrance. From the outside the building appeared to contain just the one room with the generator sitting slap bang in the middle of the concrete floor. However, there was another room set into the back wall.

Curious, I touched the padlock. It was new and there were no cobwebs around the frame which told me the door had been opened recently. Or possibly that should be regularly.

"Patty, are you coming?" Barbie's voice broke through the spell, snapping me back to the horrible reality that was Sam's disappearance.

Putting the padlocked door from my mind, I hurried after the rest of my group.

We didn't find Edward or Sam, but we did find signs of a struggle. Barbie retraced the path she believed she had taken through Edward's house when she took off after Sam. She'd seen him go, but hadn't been fast enough to follow and lost him in the confusion.

In a room decorated with soft furnishings, sofas, and a television, we found a lamp lying on its side. A magazine that had probably been on a side table had come to rest on the floor and a door that led to the garden was ajar.

"This is blood," stated Barbie, her face grim. She was in a crouch, examining a suspiciously red mark on the marble. I moved to get a closer look, but I never doubted her claim.

There were several bright red droplets, one of which had been stepped in to spread and smear it.

"Madam." Jermaine spoke to get my attention, but the sombre tone he employed shot a spike of ice through me.

He was over by the door leading to outside where he'd found something. My breath caught in my throat when I saw what it was.

With a trembling hand, I reached down to pick up Sam's magnifying glass.

The ghostly apparitions – whatever they were, had vanished into the night just as spookily as they appeared. I felt sick to my stomach to allow the thoughts to enter my head, yet I had to accept that whoever, or whatever was behind the terrifying attack, had taken Sam with them when they left.

Edward said they were coming for him, but if he'd thought such an event was imminent, there had been no outward indication. He took us to his home, and before he could fully explain why he believed he was being targeted, they had invaded his house. Unless he had evaded them and was hiding out somewhere in the forest surrounding his house, which I didn't believe he was, he was either dead or their prisoner. The same could be said about Sam and it made my chest feel like my heart had been torn out.

Deepa's voice rang out, "The police are here."

Convinced the threat had passed, Martin had allowed his wife to dress his wound and the two of them had gone outside to wait for the police. The police had access to motorised transport in the form of quad bikes – on the whole island, only the emergency services were permitted to travel at speed. Approaching the lobby, I could hear the rumbling engines outside. They shut off before I could get to the door, but just as I was stepping out of the house with Jermaine and Barbie on my heels, all hell broke loose.

5

CIGARETTE SMOKER

I heard a gun being cocked and a bark of command to, "Get on the ground!" Bright floodlights burst to life right in front of my face, blinding me in an instant. Forced to shield my face, I heard, but couldn't see the officers coming for me and was shocked to be grabbed roughly and shoved to the marble floor.

"What's going on?" I wailed, trying to get my bearings. "We called you! We were attacked!" My words were echoed and reflected by all my friends, but the cops were not inclined to listen.

Boots stormed past my eyes as more cops flooded the house, their voices filling it as they shouted for anyone inside to make themselves known. The sound of Molly's frightened voice and Gloria's cursing punctuated the cops' commands.

In less than a handful of seconds it was over, and we were all in custody. I was face down on the floor – not a place a lady should ever find herself, and I was hopping mad.

Twisting my head to find someone I could shout at, I spotted Martin and Deepa. They were on the grass, their hands cuffed behind their backs. They were not resisting, but were being treated as if they had.

"Hey!" I shouted with all the indignity I felt. "Hey, who's in charge here? Why are you arresting us?" There was a hand in the middle of my back, keeping me in place. I continued to twist my head around, trying to find someone who would answer me.

When a reply came, the voice was calm and devoid of the hurried energy all the other cops were displaying.

"You are under arrest because we are responding to a report of a break in and an attack," said a man. I turned my head to the left, looking across the lawn to find a man patiently lighting a cigarette. When the flare of the match died away, he puffed a plume of ugly blue smoke into the air and looked my way for the first time. "This is the house of Edward Teach, a prominent member of this island's community and the descendent of one of our patriarchs. I do not know you, but I find you here at the scene of a reported crime, the first person we saw upon arrival has blood on his shirt, and until it can be proven otherwise, I will continue to treat you as the criminals you most likely are."

The cops all wore black shorts and a short sleeved black dress shirt, pressed to produce impressive creases. Badges of rank and other insignia adorned their sleeves, and each had a radio pinned to their shirt over the left breast. They appeared to be exclusively male and a blend of races – the island a hodgepodge of influences over the centuries. Their weapons, drawn when they flooded across the lawn to subdue us, were back in the holsters at their hips, and though we presented no threat that I could perceive, they were not about to let us get up.

From his position on the grass, Martin barked, "We are the ones who reported the attack, you idiot. We were attacked."

The man took another draw on his cigarette, slowly and deliberately before he responded.

"No, the call we received was from Edward Teach. A second call came in, but by then we were already scrambling to respond. I will guess that one of you made the second call in a feeble attempt to cover your tracks or throw us off the scent."

Incensed, I raged, "Edward Teach met us at the dock. We stepped off the Aurelia less than an hour ago. What possible motivation could we have for attacking him?"

"He is rich," came the instant reply.

I was about to argue when someone inside the house returned to the door at speed.

"Blood, Sir. There's blood inside the house and I found most of them to be carrying weapons, Sir. There's an old lady in here with a meat cleaver in her handbag!"

The man with the cigarette sounded amused when he said, "Well, well." He flicked the butt into the darkness and strode toward the house. He was going to walk right by me, or maybe even step over me, and I had to try to make him see sense.

"Listen, please," I begged. "My name is Patricia Fisher. Please contact Alistair Huntley, he's the captain of the Aurelia and he will vouch for all of us. Some of the people here are from the ship's security team. We did not come here to hurt Edward Teach, he met us at the dock and begged me to take a case."

My final sentence did something because the cigarette smoker stopped moving. Two yards from me and halfway up the marble steps at the front of the house, he bent sideways at the waist to get a better look at my face.

"Take a case? As in investigate? Are you with law enforcement, Mrs Fisher?"

Normally I loathe that my name and face get recognised – it is rarely a positive experience, but right now I wanted him to know who I was so we could skip forward to the part where he listened to reason and let us all go.

"Yes," I replied as calmly as I could. "I have been in the newspapers, perhaps you read about the Godmother and the Alliance of Families?" I left the question hanging in the air in the hope that he would say yes. Whether he had figured out who I was or not, he chose to stay silent. Pressing on, I said, "Edward knew my name and knew to look for me coming off the Aurelia when it docked tonight. He wanted me to investigate something for him." My mouth went dry and the words coming from it petered out when I remembered one of the last things he said before the 'ghosts' turned up. He told us he hadn't gone to the police because he believed some of them were corrupt.

I tried to look at the insignia on cigarette smoker's arm, but I couldn't see it. He was clearly in charge, so he was either the local chief or something akin to that. Was he a corrupt cop? Did that explain why we were being treated so harshly?

"What, Mrs Fisher?" cigarette smoker asked with a chuckle behind his words. "What was it that Edward Teach supposedly wanted an amateur sleuth to investigate when he has access to a whole police department?" He didn't believe a word I was saying.

"He was scared someone might be trying to hurt him. He talked about local criminal gangs and worried they might try to use the legend of his family's history to cover up their crime." I was picking my words carefully, certain one mention of ghosts or zombie pirates was going to destroy any credibility I might have.

"Dead pirates, I tell you," yelled Molly from within the house. "I could see bones and one of 'em cut Martin with 'is cutlass."

I groaned and closed my eyes.

"She's not lying," added Gloria, the pair being led through the house to join the rest of us on the front lawn.

Cigarette smoker commanded, "Collect them up and take them to the station."

"Wait," I pleaded. "When we were attacked, Edward panicked and ran. One of our friends, a young man with Downs Syndrome went after him. We haven't seen either since."

I was hauled from the ground by my arms, the manoeuvre painful though I refused to show my discomfort. Once upright, I found the cigarette smoker right in my face, a broad grin splitting his lips.

"Did the ghostly pirates take them, do you think?" He was mocking me. Sam was missing, we were in custody, and I knew there was nothing I could do to change our situation. It didn't stop me from trying.

"Please, you're not listening to me. Sam is in trouble …"

"No!" Cigarette smoker roared in my face, his foul breath assailing my nostrils to make me want to gag. "You are the ones who are in trouble. I will not waste my time searching for a person who you probably just invented on the spot."

"He's my grandson!" protested Gloria.

Barking at the officers around him, cigarette smoker ordered, "Get them out of here, right now. I want them processed and in cells by the time I get back to the station. They are not allowed to make any calls until I have interviewed them. Is that understood?"

He got, "Yes, Chief," in obedient response from half a dozen men and was already striding into the house before the answers died away.

Gripped tightly around the meaty part of my upper left arm, I was pushed toward the quad bikes. I couldn't see how they were going to use those to escort us to the station – wherever it was – or how they ever took any criminal anywhere riding pillion.

My confusion lasted only as long as it took for me to notice the horse and cart arriving. Trundling slowly through the entrance gate to Edward's property, the cart itself was a cage. We were going to be shoved inside it.

My emotions were a confused jumble, anxiety fighting with fear for Sam, despair over our situation, and anger that we were being treated so terribly. The combination made me feel weak and I had to duck my head as spots started to dance before my eyes.

Incarcerated on this tiny island and denied access to a phone, we were in real trouble. So far from the rest of civilisation, the rules here were different and I had no idea what they were. Alistair would come looking for us when he realised he hadn't heard from me, but how long would that take? What was happening to Sam in the meantime?

We would get out, sure enough, but how soon I could not tell. Stuffed into the mobile jail cell, I felt nothing but misery. My friends all joined me and though we could have talked, we were all silent, each keeping our own thoughts.

When the cops hoisted Gloria up with little regard for her age, I saw the tear on her cheek. I didn't ask what it was for as my own eyes chose that moment to express their damp worry for Ensign Samuel Chalk.

6

PROFESSOR OF MARITIME ANTIQUITIES

Unbeknownst to Patricia, a man called Xavier Silvestre was looking for her. The rich Spaniard's mission to find a haul of treasure had led him to the Aurelia.

Silvestre did not think of himself as a treasure hunter, truly he had no interest in any treasure other than that associated with the San José, an 18th century treasure galleon that supposedly sunk in 1708. Loaded with gold, silver, and jewels from the mines of Columbia, the report was that it was chased and subsequently sent to the bottom by the British Navy when it refused to yield.

Silvestre held a different theory, that the captain and his officers had conspired to steal the treasure. They left the port in South America without their naval escort for protection and were never seen again. The British claimed to have sunk her, but Silvestre believed they attacked a different vessel that also went missing around that time.

His beliefs were not, of course, wildly unfounded speculation, there were clues. Artefacts had come to life over the centuries. Not many, but enough that he invested money into deeper research. If the San José treasure was out there, the fortune it represented was beyond compare in modern history.

It would be like inventing Google, Amazon, and Facebook at the same time and somehow retaining the shares to all three. Even then, the treasure in the San José's hold might still be greater in value.

Years of painstaking research and chasing down every half lead that popped up had slowly eroded his hope of ever finding it, but then a new piece was found. A man walked into a museum in Rio de Janeiro with a jewel encrusted cross in his hand. That man was dead now, killed by Silvestre once he was content there was no information left to extract.

The man's dying revelation was the location of Finn Murphy's body. Finn had uncut gems that had to come from the hold of the San José, the cross was proof for it carried the emblem of a family who were last seen boarding the ship.

Finn Murphy wasn't going to answer any questions, but Patricia Fisher had published an online newspaper article about the find and that meant she knew more than anyone else. Silvestre was going to quiz her until she revealed every scrap of information she had.

The only hurdle he faced was in finding her and getting her alone. She travelled with what could only be referred to as an entourage. A giant Jamaican man Silvestre knew to be her butler, an attractive blonde woman and several members of the ship's security team could be found in her company at any point in time. The only time she left them was when she visited her lover, the captain of the ship.

That might have presented an opportunity were it not for the inconvenient fact that their rendezvous were often in the captain's quarters high on the bridge. There was no way Silvestre could see to get to them there and her butler accompanied her to the bridge elevator each time where he handed her off to an armed guard.

After days of studying her movements, Silvestre knew his best and possibly only chance was going to come on land when she left the ship for a spot of tourism.

He was going to find her shortly, but had found it necessary to fake his departure from the ship and reboard it wearing a new disguise. Altering his appearance was a skill he proudly employed on a regular basis. If Patricia Fisher had spotted him before, then she would recognise a scruffy surfer-looking man with long blonde hair and a large moustache. Those features were now gone and he'd shaved his head, and donned an expensive hand-cut suit.

He was now playing the part of Professor Noriega, the San José expert from the Museum of Brazil in Rio.

Professor Noriega was dead, of course, murdered by Silvestre to cover his tracks and ensure no one else knew about the cross or the possibility that the San José might have been found. Silvestre was uncharacteristically pleased with his latest disguise for it afforded him a genuine reason for seeking out Patricia Fisher.

Her published article about the treasure made her an obvious choice for someone with Professor Noriega's reputation to want to meet. He was going to stride boldly onto the Aurelia with his new identification – his assistant had dispatched new fake documents to be waiting when they docked – and with luck would be able to politely request access to the jewels and Mrs Fisher.

If it didn't work, he would start killing people, but though the gentle approach came with risks, he was willing to give it a chance to succeed first.

However, as expected, Patricia Fisher had gone ashore. He discovered this when he announced himself to a member of crew and explained why he was on board.

"I really need to speak with her most urgently," Silvestre explained in a faux embarrassed manner. "Sorry, it's really important to me. This is my life's work, you see. If I could just get a message to her."

The ship was going to be exactly where it was for another twenty-four hours. If he could complete his work before it sailed, he could move on to wherever the information he gathered took him. The point was to stay on the trail. The chance of being caught out might be slim, but it increased with every day he remained on board.

Lieutenant Reynolds chose his response carefully. He needed to be polite and helpful – the man was a passenger, but he wasn't about to give away another passenger's information, most especially not that of the quasi-celebrity, Patricia Fisher.

"If you give me your details, Sir: cabin number, a phone or email by which you might be contactable, I will be sure to pass them on." He delivered the offer with a warm smile.

Silvestre knew not to push his luck.

"That would be most helpful, thank you. Can I ask, the report she published spoke of a stowaway who was found to have uncut gemstones in his belly. If I cannot yet speak with Patricia Fisher, perhaps it will be possible to inspect the cadaver and the gems? Normally, this is work I would have a research assistant perform, but time is of the essence and this discovery could be of vital historic importance." A master of manipulation, Silvestre was using all his guile to get that which he needed. The crew was there to help, and Silvestre knew his credentials looked genuine because he paid a small fortune to keep a counterfeiter on his pay role.

Unable to think of a reason to deny the request, Lieutenant Reynolds said, "Give me a moment, please, Sir." He stepped away, leaning down to activate the radio pinned to his lapel.

He knew the body was still in the morgue and that the jewels were somewhere on board the ship. The discovery of a dead stowaway was news enough that the crew was still talking about it. That he was found with a knife sticking out of his chest and had clearly been murdered only increased the speculation surrounding his death. Then add that the autopsy revealed a fortune in the man's abdomen, and it was all the crew was talking about.

Quite why Mrs Fisher had chosen to tell the world via an online newspaper, Lieutenant Reynolds could not fathom, but the facts were out there and now he had a professor of maritime antiquities begging to be allowed to examine the evidence.

Deep in the ship's lower decks where the central sickbay with its small operating theatre and morgue were located, Dr Hideki Nakamura answered the radio.

7

ACCUSED

At the police station, not far from the harbour where our nightmarish adventure began, the cops processed us one at a time, keeping us separated as best they could.

They took my possessions: phone, handbag, and everything else. I wanted to call Alistair and begged to be allowed to make at least one supervised phone call. The desk sergeant processing my paperwork looked to a colleague.

"Chief Quimby said no calls until he has interviewed them." The reply was good enough for the sergeant who took my phone and placed it into a bag.

"I have dogs on board the ship," I complained. "I only want to alert someone to deal with them."

The sergeant didn't even look up. "No calls."

Denied, my entire attitude changed. "Have you any idea how many human rights violations you are committing right now? Do you? What do you think is going to happen when the captain of the Aurelia finds out what happened to us? This island needs tourism to support its economy. The lawsuits I am going to slam this department with are going to make a hurricane look like a mild afternoon breeze ..."

"Put her in cell three," he grumbled.

The cop standing by my left shoulder made to grab my arm, and I yanked it away.

"Are you listening to anything I am saying."

The cop to my left didn't miss a second time, gripping my arm with more force than was necessary – I mean, where could I go?

Finally, the sergeant looked up. "How many human rights violations? No idea. Do you?"

I didn't have the first clue and my mouth flapped open and closed as I tried to form my next sentence.

"Cell three," he repeated, and I was hauled away, a second cop stepping in to take my right arm.

I tried to dig my feet in, but the men holding my arms were too strong.

Rage distorted Jermaine's face and Barbie shouted, "Hey! Leave her alone! We haven't done anything wrong!"

Her cries were echoed by the rest of my friends, but the cops were not listening. Edward's claim there might be corrupt officers among them sounded more plausible all the time.

Dragged through the doorway, the last thing I heard was the sergeant bellowing for my protesting friends to remain silent.

Hours passed.

I was stuck in my cell and full of the worry of a mother with a missing child. Not that Sam was my son, but he filled a spot in my heart that might otherwise have been dedicated to my own child or children if I had any.

When the sound of someone in the corridor stopped outside my cell door and the little hatch at eye height opened, I swung my legs off my bed. I had no idea what time it might be, only that I had fallen asleep at some point, and it was still dark outside the tiny window above my head.

I was drenched with sweat, the humidity of the island competing with the buzzing, biting insects to see who could be most annoying. Feeling scuzzy, but relieved when I heard the key go into my lock, I got to my feet and waited.

The person outside was yet another man – I was yet to see a woman in uniform – and he was not one I had seen before.

"Come along," he beckoned. He waited for me to exit the cell, indicating that I should stand against the opposite wall while he closed and locked my cell.

Expecting that I was now to be taken to an interview room – it's not my first time getting arrested – I was not disappointed. While it filled me with no joy to see Chief Quimby again, I was glad to be able to face my accuser.

"What did you do with Edward Teach?" he demanded to know before the door even closed behind me. Chief Quimby's gaze was unwavering, his eyes locked on my face as I walked to the chair set opposite his, brushed some imaginary crumbs from it, and sat down.

I would not label myself as an old hand at this game, but I'm no newbie either. He wanted to control the interview and I wasn't going to give him a chance.

"Did you find Samuel Chalk?" I asked when I had made myself comfortable.

Chief Quimby jolted in his chair like it had delivered an electric shock. Jerking forward so he was leaning halfway across the table separating us, he slammed a fist down with a loud bang.

"I'm asking the questions!"

Calmly, I replied, "Which I will answer if you pose any that are relevant, and in return update me on the missing member of my team."

Catching himself before he could shout another reply, Chief Quimby snorted a forced laugh through his nose and relaxed his posture. I'd made him dance to my tune and had taken the upper hand. He knew it and was savvy enough to counter me by controlling his temper.

"You have no room to negotiate, Mrs Fisher. I can charge you and everyone in your 'team' with breaking and entering, burglary …"

"Burglary?" I questioned, mockingly. "How do you propose to pull that off?"

"They were carrying knives which by their own admission they took from Mr Teach's house. That's burglary. Anyone involved in law enforcement, even from such a fringe position as yours, ought to know that."

He was being ridiculous, and I doubted he would even try to make it stick, but it was not a point worth arguing.

Changing tack, I asked, "Are you planning to charge us, Chief Quimby? Do you believe you can secure a conviction?"

To avoid answering, he said, "My detectives are still gathering evidence. Now, I want to know what you did with Edward Teach, Mrs Fisher, and you are not going to leave this room or this police station until you tell me."

"Then we have a stalemate, Chief Quimby, for I have already told you what happened. He met us at the docks, invited me to investigate his concerns that a local criminal gang might wish him harm, and begged that we accompany him to his house. He offered a considerable sum for my time, and at the house he was trying to explain who might be targeting him and why when we were attacked."

"By ghostly pirates," Chief Quimby filled in the rest of my sentence though I'd had no intention of saying the words myself.

With a tired smile, I said, "I think we can assume it was a clever ruse to hide the attackers' real identity. It worked too for I would not be able to identify one of them."

"Some of your friends appear to believe they were real."

He hadn't asked a question, so I didn't feel a need to respond. Instead, I asked again about Sam, this time softening my voice to make it sound like I was pleading for information.

Annoyed, he snapped, "I have no idea what might have happened to him, but here is my guess." I was all ears. "I think you are telling the truth about being hired, but Edward Teach is not your client. I believe you are here to kidnap him, and I am in the process of having your precious ship impounded. The missing member of your team escaped with Edward Teach while the rest of you ran interference to ensure he got back to the ship."

Unable to believe my ears, my jaw fell open. "You are barking mad."

"Am I, Mrs Fisher? By your own admission, you were after money – that's why you took the job."

"No, that's not what I …"

"You left the ship and went immediately to the home of Edward Teach."

"He invited us to go with him."

"So you claim, but there are no witnesses to back up your statement. Your accomplices claim you took rickshaws to reach Edward Teach's house, my officers have canvased the local rickshaw drivers and none of them took that route last night. You are lying, Mrs Fisher."

I could only frown, my forehead creasing as I tried to make sense of what I was hearing. It would be easy to assume Chief Quimby was lying, but I could not think of a reason why he would. Last night he claimed they were responding to a call from Edward, not us, and the time it took them to get to his house suggested that could be true – they arrived too soon after Deepa called them. They had to have already been on their way. Now the rickshaw drivers were lying too?

Chief Quimby persisted, "Why didn't you take rickshaws to get there, Mrs Fisher? Eh? To make sure there were no witnesses, that's why. If Edward Teach is on board the Aurelia, my men will find him and you and everyone in your 'team' will be charged with kidnapping. I find it interesting that you call them your team. It's like they were hired to do a job. Most people refer to their close acquaintances as friends."

"They are my friends," I argued. "But we all work together and …"

He waved a dismissive hand. "You can stop now, Mrs Fisher. I am bored of your lies."

Trying hard to keep the rising anger I felt under control, I came forward in my chair.

"Look. Every moment you spend investigating any possible link I might have to Edward's disappearance is time you are wasting. If Edward and Sam are still alive, and Lord knows I pray they are, then they are in trouble."

Chief Quimby looked me square in the eye. "You're really not going to tell me what you did with him, are you? You're really going to make me gather all the evidence and prove your guilt, aren't you? This is going to go so much worse for you if you refuse to cooperate, Mrs Fisher."

I closed my mouth and accepted defeat. He wasn't going to listen no matter what I said. The interview was terminated a short while later, the same cop returning to take me back to my cell.

More time passed and I fell asleep at some point on the uncomfortable wooden bed with its almost pointless mattress. I was woken by the sound of a key in my door and found the same cop as before when the door swung open. With me walking ahead of him, he directed me back to the processing room where I found the same desk sergeant still sitting behind his desk.

He had my things laid out on the desk.

"Am I being released?" I asked, hope blooming in my chest.

"Check your belongings and sign here," the sergeant instructed without answering my question or bothering to look up.

Someone had come to my rescue. That was the message bouncing around in my head. Hoping I was going to find Alistair when I got outside, I held back the torrent of smart comments I had for the officers around me. I truly wanted to unleash everything in my arsenal, but held my tongue knowing it would do me no good to say what I thought.

Snatching up my phone, I checked to see if there were any missed calls from Sam, or a message perhaps to let me know he was all right. There was nothing, so ignoring the sergeant who wanted me to sign for my things, I dialled Sam's number and put my phone to my ear.

It went straight to voicemail, crushing me once again.

Led through a different door to the one we came through the previous evening, I found myself in the police station's main reception area. The sound of raised voices, muffled but unmistakable, filled the air.

The door closed behind me, leaving me without an escort at last. I was by myself, ignored except for a single glance by the officer behind the reception desk, and needed to ask where my friends were.

"Patty!"

At the sound of Barbie's voice, I spun around to look out through the station's entrance. She was in the street outside along with everyone else. They were all looking my way now, Barbie waving madly so I would see her.

Gathered beneath a streetlamp, my friends looked sleep-deprived, and their clothes were rumpled. Even Jermaine looked less than impeccable. Gloria was sitting on the low wall that bordered the road, but my hope that Sam might have been found during the night and returned to us was immediately dashed.

I started toward the doors, but didn't get to them before the sound of the argument to my rear increased in volume – someone had opened a door, the noise from inside a room spilling out. The additional clarity now that the voices were less muffled jabbed my brain with a single piece of vital information: it was Alistair I could hear.

Spinning around again, I was facing the reception desk when a door to its right flew open, my boyfriend displaying his emotions physically.

I saw no sign of Chief Quimby, but tailing Alistair was a tall, black man in a fine suit. He was a little pudgy around the hips, and his hair had receded to form an inch wide ring of short white bristles above his ears. I placed him in his sixties and guessed that he was a lawyer.

Alistair saw me and stopped speaking mid-sentence.

"Patricia!" He rushed to me, sweeping me into a hug and holding me tight.

The desk cop behind reception, glanced up again before going back to whatever he was doing, and the lawyer/whoever he was waited to one side, looking away rather than watch our embrace.

More than ten seconds passed as we held each other, and when Alistair pulled away it was so he could place his hands either side of my face and pull me into a kiss.

"Darling," he whispered, looking down at me with a heart

wrenching expression of love. "You stink."

I jolted. I hadn't misheard him though and he was chuckling at me now.

"We need to get you back to the ship and clean you up," he hissed too softy for anyone but me to hear. The rest of your friends don't smell any better." Twisting to look at the man in the sharp suit, Alistair spoke at normal conversation volume, "Mayor Boxley, this is Patricia Fisher."

The mayor advanced, extending his hand to take mine.

"Angus," he introduced himself and dipped his head to kiss my hand. "Mrs Fisher, I wish to extend my personal apology for all that has befallen you since your arrival. I can assure you there will be a full enquiry into Chief Quimby's behaviour, and his men will be dedicating their time to finding the missing member of your group. I have insisted he cancel all leave and call in every officer under his control."

He released my hand which fell back to my side. "That's very good of you, Angus. Thank you for coming here in person too. I'm sure your influence helped to get us released." I was being generous because it was the polite thing to do, and his reply surprised me.

"Oh, that's very generous of you, but I was here anyway, I'm afraid. One of my staff has gone missing. An accountant. It's probably nothing, but ..."

He didn't feel a need to finish his sentence and that suited me because I had questions I wanted him to answer. "Do you have any idea what could have happened to Edward? He believed he was being targeted by a local criminal gang, but the attack at his house happened before he was able to tell us who that was or what he had done to warrant such interest."

The mayor shrugged deeply, turning his bottom lip out in a universally recognised expression for 'Who can say?'.

"I'm sorry, Mrs Fisher. I am as in the dark as everyone else. I had very few dealings with Edward. He has become something of a recluse since his father died. In fact, I'm genuinely unsure when we last were in the same room together." Mayor Boxley delivered his reply, but as he was doing so, I could see the wheels turning inside his head. "You are proposing to find out what happened to him, aren't you, Mrs Fisher? Your reputation precedes you, but I must caution against beginning an investigation that may interfere with Chief Quimby's."

I almost told him what he could do with Chief Quimby's investigation. Managing to tailor my reply, I said, "A very dear friend of mine went missing last night. I am not leaving this island without him." I meant every word and would appeal to the Maharaja to buy the entire nation if I thought it would help. I was going to find Sam, and no power on earth was going to stop me.

Looking concerned now, the mayor lowered his voice, "Mrs Fisher, this is most ill advised. I know Chief Quimby treated you harshly, but crime here is rare because he is a slick operator. He will get to the bottom of what happened. Now that he is no longer considering you as a suspect, he can turn his full attention to finding out who is responsible."

Through gritted teeth, I snarled, "I don't care. I don't care what you think or who you put on this case. I am getting Sam back and anyone who gets in my way had better watch out."

I was talking like John Wayne and feeling fuelled with enough righteousness to smash through walls if I had to.

Startled by my choice of words and my attitude, Mayor Boxley took a small step back. He was going to say something else, but Alistair cut him off.

"I suggest you advise Chief Quimby to do precisely as she says and stay out of her way, Angus. Patricia makes global headlines for good reason. If she gets Sam back, I might be prepared to let this incident pass without reporting it to the cruise line – I'm sure you wouldn't want to be the elected official who killed the nation's tourism income." The threat was left hanging as Alistair turned toward the door and showed me a smile. "After you, darling."

I flicked my eyes in the mayor's direction, but he looked away, unwilling to meet the challenge of my gaze. We were done with the police station, and it was time to start investigating. I wanted to get stuck in straight away, but there was a small matter to take care of first.

8

BREAKFAST WITH A KILLER

We were back on board the Aurelia and in my suite where Lieutenant Kashmir had spent the night in one of the spare bedrooms. He expressed concern at the length of our absence and reported it was he who alerted Alistair when we failed to return the previous evening as planned.

Anna and Georgie were pleased to see me, fussing around my feet, and jumping at my legs when I first returned. They followed me into my bedroom where I showered speedily. I would have forgone such daily ablutions had my boyfriend not remarked on my personal odour, such was my desire to start looking for Sam. Admittedly, I was uncomfortable in my clothes; they had taken on that sticky, clammy effect one gets after wearing them in the heat for too long.

Feeling fresh, clean, and imbued with a desire to get back out there, I dressed in a hurry and went to find breakfast. Leaving my bedroom with a towel in my hands as I continued to pat my hair dry, the dachshunds trotted gamely after me, undoubtedly thinking it must be breakfast time.

It was still early for breakfast, but I was going to eat – notably dinner never happened last night – so it would have been wrong to deny them.

Jermaine appeared through the door that led to his butler's annex before I could get to the kitchen. He was already dressed in full butler's livery, making me roll my eyes and sigh.

"Jermaine, sweetie, I know you love being my butler …"

"What is a man without purpose, madam?"

This was an old argument I saw no need to reiterate. He was never going to change with me pushing him to do so. I had learned to accept that he was happy as my butler and wanted little more in life than to keep me safe and well cared for.

"I'm just saying you didn't need to get all dressed up to serve me breakfast, sweetie. You are coming ashore with me again, yes?"

"Naturally, madam."

"Then you will need to change into something more fitting for kicking people in the ear."

"Who's getting kicked in the ear?" asked Barbie, exiting her bedroom – one of five inside the Windsor Suite in which I resided on board the Aurelia. In the same time that I'd had to get showered and changed, she'd managed to produce absolute perfection. Dressed in black Lycra, she'd applied a swipe of mascara and dried her hair so it fell in glorious, shiny, blonde locks.

I looked down at myself. My top was rumpled and had damp marks on it where I'd dried in a hurry, the laces of one running shoe were untied and trailing on the carpet. I wasn't wearing any makeup and my hair was still wet.

Frowning, I asked, "How do you do that?"

Barbie looked genuinely mystified when she replied, "Do what?"

"Breakfast, madam?" asked Jermaine, taking out the box of doggy chow for me to feed Anna and Georgie. They wagged their tails and looked excited as only a hungry dog can.

Barbie jogged by me to get to the kitchen, opening the refrigerator and grabbing a carton of milk.

"Yes, breakfast. I'm starving." She poured milk into a tall glass and chugged the lot.

We settled on ham omelettes and toast, Barbie insisting we

needed the carbs today. I offered no argument – she never lets me have toast.

While Jermaine prepared our food, I messaged the rest of the team, using my phone rather than my radio. I wasn't sure where I had put it before I left the ship yesterday and didn't want to admit it.

Barbie was on her phone too, retrieving it from a pouch on her hip when it pinged. I figured it was probably a message from her boyfriend Hideki. He had been working last night and unable to join us, but provided he wasn't too fatigued from working the night shift – he couldn't be any more exhausted than the rest of us - I expected to see him today.

My phone pinged in my hand as responses came back. Deepa and Martin were on their way, so too Schneider and Pippin, the other two members of my security team who had chosen to remain on board last night. They'd missed all the excitement, but were keen to join the hunt for Sam now.

Molly I included only because she had been involved last night. She wasn't assigned to me as part of my team – I have four officers who help me deal with crimes committed on board the ship, but as my former housemaid, she knew me and my friends better than anyone else on board. Not including her would have been a snub.

The dogs finished chasing kibble around their bowls and looked up at me with expectant expressions – they wanted milk.

Jermaine had the carton in his hand when I looked, his arm extended in my direction even though his focus was still on the omelettes.

With them lapping at the milk in a single bowl, their feverish actions reminding me of the child's game 'Hungry Hippos', I thought about whether to include Gloria. There could be no way of knowing what today might bring. We might need to move fast. Heck we might get chased; it's not like that would be unusual. In her eighties, was it fair to bring her into that environment? Conversely, was it okay to leave her out just because she is a little older than the rest of us? If I looked at the average age of the group, I was two decades older. No one would think to discount me, but before I could pick up my phone and call Sam's Gran, I heard a knock at the door and Gloria calling through it.

"Cooeee! Only me."

Barbie called, "I'll get it," twisting her head to see how Jermaine would react. She got a narrowing of his eyes that suggested she had better not dare and she giggled at her friend. Jermaine took his butler's duties very seriously and no one was permitted to answer the door if he was there to do it.

Jermaine deftly served omelettes, tore off his apron, and walked at a butler's pace to let Gloria in.

She was not the only one outside.

Hideki was there too.

"Babes!" Barbie leapt off her stool at the kitchen's breakfast bar and bounced across the room to leap into his arms. Her legs wrapped around his back, the impact of her lean muscular body enough to make him stagger a pace.

He looped his arms under her buttocks to support her weight and walked into my suite with her clamped to his torso. She was kissing his face and neck with the carefree abandon only a woman in her late teens or early twenties can muster. It was only when Jermaine shut the door and I could hear him speaking to someone that I looked to see who else might have arrived.

Between Gloria and the Hideki/Barbie hybrid, the view to my door was blocked, only Jermaine's head visible above theirs.

Jermaine called out, "Madam, are you available to receive guests?"

I had to quickly chew and swallow the piece of toast in my mouth, peering around the new arrivals to see who it was. Clearly it was someone I didn't know, or Jermaine would not feel the need to announce them.

Hideki chose that moment to drop Barbie back to the carpet, prising his face away from hers so he could speak.

"This is Professor Noriega," the ship's junior doctor announced. "He's from the Museum of Brazil in Rio de Janeiro where he works in maritime antiquities."

I didn't have time for pleasantries; I barely had time for breakfast. The only thing I wanted to do with my day was find Sam, but the man was already in my suite, and I knew why he was here.

Abandoning my meal, I slid off my stool to go to him. Acting as if that were a cue, Jermaine closed my door and Professor Noriega started toward me. We met in the middle of the room.

"Mrs Fisher, thank you so much for seeing me," he gushed excitedly. "I cannot sufficiently explain what excitement it brought my department when we read your report of the gems you found. Please," he thrust an arm back toward the kitchen, "do not let your meal ruin on my account. I shall be only too happy to wait."

My stomach grumbled, reminding me how empty it was. I let his hand go and returned to my seat, talking as I walked.

"The truth is that I didn't publish that article, Professor. Someone hacked my computer and did it for me in an attempt to cause me embarrassment."

Silvestre didn't say it, but the news came as no surprise. He'd read into the woman he was stalking and couldn't understand how she had come to do something so clumsy. It seemed completely out of character. Now he knew how it had happened.

Everyone was buying his disguise without question. He didn't consider himself to be a master of accents, but experience had taught him that whenever anyone questioned whatever accent he employed, it was easy to dismiss their concerns by saying he was brought up by parents who travelled a lot. He doubted anyone in the room was attuned enough to notice his Rio accent was less than perfect.

To respond to the English sleuth's claim, he said, "Goodness gracious. Someone hacked you? Have they been caught?"

I paused my forkful of omelette halfway to my mouth to say, "Not yet." I swallowed quickly so I could ask, "What is it that brings you here, Professor Noriega?"

"Call me Julio, please," he insisted. I didn't reply because I was eating, and he ploughed onward. "I came to see the jewels, Mrs Fisher."

"Patricia, please, Julio," I replied between bites.

I got a nod of acknowledgement. "Patricia, yes. As your good friend the doctor just revealed, I study maritime antiquities and the discovery of uncut gems intrigued me. It is entirely possible they come from a shipwreck – I'm sure you know there were many treasure ships carrying gold and jewels from the new world back to Europe a few centuries ago. To be certain I need to examine the stones, but I also wish to learn all that you know about the man they were found inside. Were there any other artefacts found with him? Anything that might give an indication that they were from a shipwreck?"

Now, I can't say what it was about the professor; whether it was the fervour with which his questions were posed, or the fact that I couldn't figure out how he would connect some uncut gems to the possibility of them leading to a long lost ship wrecked centuries ago, but I chose to lie.

I did so quickly, swallowing the piece of still-too-hot omelette without chewing so no one around me could answer first and tell him the truth.

"No. Goodness, no nothing like that? What sort of thing might be considered an artefact? All we found was the poor chap's body." It was true that we found Finn Murphy devoid of possessions, heck he didn't even have a wallet or passport on him to tell us who he was, but a few days after his body came to light, we found where he'd been sleeping.

Barbie twitched upon hearing the lie leave my mouth, but she didn't argue – we had all agreed the priceless horde had to be kept as secret as possible. Just a handful of us knew it even existed. Keeping it that way relied upon everyone pretending they knew nothing about it.

A tatty, threadbare, smelly sleeping bag had lain next to an equally ratty knapsack. In the knapsack we found his passport – the key to unlocking the identity of the man in our morgue, but that wasn't the only thing tucked inside the dead man's luggage. There were a few tins of food and several million dollars' worth of gold coins and jewels.

We had discussed that we needed expert help to identify the items and their origin, so on the face of it, Professor Noriega was the perfect person to be truthful with. It was not our intention to keep the treasure, but a man had died for it, and I wanted to know why. It was my job to know why.

"He's seen the body already," Hideki chipped in. "Lieutenant Reynolds brought him down to sickbay. I couldn't see a reason to deny him access."

"Yes," said the professor. "That's another reason why I wondered if there might be more to this than just a few gemstones. Why was he murdered and what secret did he die protecting?"

"You mean other than the jewels he'd chosen to swallow?" I fixed the professor with an expression that did nothing to hide my curiosity.

He was shorter than average at perhaps five feet and eight inches. Though I knew he would measure his height using the metric system, I was a feet and inches kind of gal and always would be. His perfectly bald head looked to be freshly shaved and his eyes behind a pair of designer spectacles were a deep brown colour the shade of polished walnut. His features were forgettable, which is not intended to be a harsh criticism, just an observation. What I mean is there was very little about him that was memorable.

"Of course," the professor laughed at himself. "I am speculating – hardly the behaviour expected of an academic. Mrs Fisher, I really wish to do a deep dive into everything you know about the victim and the circumstances of his death…"

I held up a hand to cut him off. It was a little rude, but he could see I was shovelling food into my mouth in a hurried fashion.

"I'm sorry, Julio. I have urgent business to which I must attend. We all do." I indicated the people around me. "Perhaps in a few days, when we are on our way to Rio, I will be able to make time for you. It just isn't possible now." I was ending the conversation because I had to. Sam was out there somewhere, and he was alive. My heart insisted I believe that and nothing short of finding his body was going to convince me otherwise.

The professor would have to have been blind to fail to read the signs, and thankfully with a bow he took a step back.

"I am intruding. I apologise."

"If this were any other time ..." I remarked. "Jermaine will see you out. Please tell him what cabin you are in. If I can make time for you, I will."

I wasn't lying; I wanted to talk to him. There was something about him that didn't quite ... I couldn't come up with a word to use. Whatever it was, I wanted to know more about him. I meet altogether too many people who are not quite who they say they are or are acting in a certain way due to a motivating factor they have chosen to conceal. I could not say for certain that he fell into that category, but something was tickling the back of my skull.

I watched, my eyes pinched together in thought while Jermaine showed Professor Julio Noriega to the door and closed it behind him.

With my breakfast gone and the last of our team messaging they would meet us on the quayside, there was no reason to stay on the ship and every reason to leave. I didn't have a lot to go on, not even a name. Edward's housemaid who recently quit – finding her was my first task. She might know something, and I hoped that we might be able to ascertain the name and identity of the local gang Edward suggested might be targeting him.

Going up against yet another criminal gang on their own turf was right at the bottom of my list of fun things to do, but someone had Sam and I would put myself and my other friends in harm's way to get him back.

"Are we off then?" asked Gloria.

I slid off my stool. "Yes. Are you sure you want to come with us? I have no idea what might happen today, but it seems likely we are going to meet some rough people and we may yet find ourselves tangling with the police again."

"The police?" she questioned, looking about to see if she was the only one confused about their position. "I thought they were on our side now? Didn't you say the mayor told the chief to find my Sam?"

I huffed out a trouble breath. "I did say that, but I'm not confident the mayor has enough sway to make it happen. Remember

Edward said there might be corrupt elements within the police department?"

Gloria looked down at the floor and dredged her memory. "Oh. Yes, he did say that, didn't he?"

"I was told not to investigate. The mayor made it sound like a warning that might have dire consequences if disobeyed."

"What a load of rhubarb," Gloria spat. "They should welcome all the help they can get."

"Not if they are in on it." My comment got the attention of everyone in the room. "How did they get to us so fast last night?" My question was aimed at everyone, but I didn't need them to answer. "Chief Quimby claimed Edward called them several minutes before Deepa reported the attack. Either he is lying – I don't see how I can prove it either way – or he is telling the truth, in which case I am really confused about what is going on."

No one said anything for several seconds and the room was quiet enough that I could hear the clock ticking on the wall in the living space.

Anna yipped, wanting my attention.

I crouched to pet her, and from the corner of my eye saw Gloria pick up her handbag.

"Gloria, what have you got in there?" I asked, with a sigh. I already knew the answer before she reached inside to remove the object weighing it down.

"My attitude adjuster," she quipped with a grin.

"No house bricks," I insisted. Gloria had a habit of carrying something solid in her handbag in case she needed to hit someone with it.

She stuck out her bottom lip. "Why not?"

"Because you'll give someone brain damage," I pointed out the obvious.

It drew a chuckle from her. "Not if I hits 'em in the trousers." She nudged Molly who sniggered too.

I rolled my eyes, and insisted, "No house bricks."

9

FREAK WEATHER

The sun was only just rising as we made our way onto the quayside. Molly, Schneider, and Pippin were waiting for us somewhere, but a thick blanket of fog had descended in the hour we had been on the ship and if they were here, we could not see them.

"What's with this mist?" asked Barbie.

"Barbie? Is that you?" Schneider's unmistakable Austrian accent rumbled through the impenetrable curtain.

My blonde friend pirouetted around to face the direction his voice came from.

"Yes. Where are you?"

"Over here." He appeared through the gloom. "This weather is crazy."

"I've never seen anything like it," remarked Molly, appearing through the mist behind Schneider. Pippin was with her.

Schneider said, "We've just been asking one of the dock workers about it. He said they get this all the time at this time of the year. Something to do with a cold current hitting warm air and being forced to rise as it climbs to get over the land. According to the guy I was talking to, this can last hours or days."

I held my hand at arm's length, wiggling my fingers. Okay, so I could see my hand in front of my face, but I could not see much beyond the end of my arm. My fingers created swirls in the misty air as I moved them.

My phone rang in my back pocket. I'd chosen to go without a handbag today out of worry that I might find myself given cause to run. Taking it out, I found Alistair's name displayed.

"Patricia," he said my name the moment the call connected. "Where are you?"

"I'm on the quayside, darling. We all are. We are just about to set off."

"Give me two minutes. I'm coming with you."

The call cut off, but the news was good. Anyone extra was welcome though Alistair and I had discussed the concept of flooding the island with teams from the crew and dismissed it. It would just cause problems with the locals and ultimately work against us. With the police far from on our side, we were better off staying under the radar. Deploying more teams was a tactic we could employ later if the need arose.

Barbie asked, "So what's the plan, Patty? We have a big team for once."

She wasn't wrong. The headcount reached double figures; I'd never had so many friends by my side. It sort of made me feel invincible and that was a welcome emotion because my heart had been aching with worry since Sam vanished.

"We should split up," suggested Martin before I could say it myself. "In two teams we can cover more ground."

Molly raised her hand. "Okay, but where are we going? I know it's a small island, but there's still a lot of territory to cover. Did I miss the part where we have any idea where to look?"

"No, Molly, you didn't miss it," I huffed with concern again. "We don't know where Sam might be. We don't know much at all. We know Edward had a maid who quit just a couple of days ago and we know he believed he was being targeted by a local criminal gang though we are not sure why yet. We need to find that housemaid and any other people who have worked for Edward in the recent past – they might know more than they realise. We need to know who the gang is. If they came after Edward, then they have Sam. If we know where he is, we can get him back."

"How?" asked Barbie, with a face that betrayed her worry. "Are we going to raid a criminal gang's lair and take him by force?"

Her question raised a valid point and the faces around me reflected her concern. What were we supposed to do if we knew who had Sam, but they refused to give him back? Admitting he was in their 'care' would implicate them in a crime and also finger them for the attack at Edward's house.

The police might not care about Sam, but I was willing to bet Chief Quimby's interest in Edward's whereabouts was genuine. Whoever had Sam would lie, and they wouldn't willingly give him back, I felt certain.

Biting my bottom lip because I knew no one was going to like my reply, I said, "Yes. If I have to. It's Sam," I added. Obviously, I wasn't talking about carrying machine guns and kicking down doors. I didn't really know what I was saying, but I knew I wouldn't leave the island without Sam at my side and could not be sure what limits I might go to.

The sound of feet on the gangplank drew our eyes that way, Alistair appearing through the mist moments later, with a wave to everyone.

He got a chorus of, "Good morning, Sirs," from the members of his crew, and flapped his waving arm at them to shut them up.

"I am leading this operation, understood? A member of our crew is missing ashore and what I ought to be doing as the captain is liaising with the police. Given the time-sensitive nature of this case, I feel my efforts are best expended in the physical pursuit of Ensign Chalk. To that end, I am ordering you all to do everything within legal bounds to find him."

I knew what he was doing, and it wasn't what he said. He knew we were probably going to get ourselves into trouble today. I had already butted heads with the local police chief and was left with the distinct impression he would happily arrest me again. All he needed was an excuse and Alistair knew I was setting out to create one.

Alistair ought to be contacting Purple Star to have them weigh in on our behalf, but those were gears that turned slowly and would do nothing to help us find Sam. My young assistant could be hurt, and he had to be frightened. We could not risk waiting for the police to do their jobs, and Alistair knew that if we created an embarrassing situation for Purple Star, they would come looking for someone to blame.

They would take our jobs. Mine, Martin's, Deepa's … everyone's. But not if we were operating under Alistair's command. If he was with us, he could claim it was his operation and we were all following orders. He would take the fall to save the rest of us and that was why he was joining us now.

That was the kind of man he was. No wonder I loved him.

He came closer to me, and I found his hand with mine.

The moment of silence that followed Alistair's words was broken when Martin spoke.

"Two teams then. How about Deepa and I take Schneider and Pippin?"

I didn't think it mattered how we split the team so long as we got on with it.

"I will accompany you," volunteered Alistair while performing a quick headcount. "That makes a five and a six."

I tugged at his hand, bringing his face down to mine.

"Good luck. Stay in contact," I murmured around a kiss.

We split, the two teams forming. We had our phones and radios with which to stay in touch, and separate areas of the town to target. I wanted to return to Edward's house – there could be clues there to find. How did the 'ghosts' get inside? How did they vanish? What route did they take to escape the grounds? There might be footprints or an obvious trail of flattened grass leading away from the house. I wouldn't know until I got there.

That was for later. First, I was going to start quizzing locals and I wasn't going to stop until I could identify and track down Edward's housemaid. I was guessing, but it made sense that she would be a resident of Torruga.

Torruga is the largest town on the island though still far too small to be considered a city. The harbour is the focal point of the whole island, and the next sizeable settlement is more than a mile beyond the town's outer limits. It was geography rather than any other factor that dictated where the town stopped expanding – the slopes became mountains too steep for anyone to consider building on.

Were Sam and Edward still in Torruga? I had no idea, but striding forward into the mist, I was going to find out.

10

ALL PRICES NEGOTIABLE

Before we even got clear of the quayside, I spotted a figure through the mist and made a beeline for it. I would quiz everyone on the island if I had to.

"Hey! Hello!" I called after the shadow as it disappeared into the swirling fog once more. My friends added their voices, the murky outline of a person pausing so we could catch up.

Ahead, I could make out the vague outline of a building and there were several brighter areas of mist where lights inside were trying to shine through.

"Good morning," beamed the figure, smiling our way as we approached. "You've just come off the ship and need pirate costumes, yes? You've come to the right man. Freddie will fix you up. I have the best range of festival outfits in my store. Step right this way."

I didn't want a costume, but the man was talking, and I was willing to play along.

"Wonderful," I gushed. "Please lead the way." I could almost see the man rubbing his hands together as he counted the potential profit from his early morning catch.

"You will not be disappointed, I assure you," he assured us.

Freddie, dressed in fancy pirate gear complete with over-the-knee boots and a feathered hat, jabbered almost non-stop. He was the first person we had come across and since I couldn't yet see anyone else, I was going to squeeze him for information.

"Freddie, how well do you know this town and the people of it?"

He flashed me a smile.

"Freddie is very popular. Everyone knows Freddie. They all come to me to buy their pirate clothes and everything else they need. I know everyone in this town."

An obvious boast and unlikely to be anywhere near true, I nevertheless suspected he was going to know enough to get me started.

"How well do you know Edward Teach, Freddie?"

"Ah, yes, Mr Edward. He is a very well-known person on this island. His family is the most famous outside of my own." He laughed to show me he was making a joke. Then he switched tack, talking over me because he wanted to focus our minds on his goods and not on my questions. "There are still two days of partying left. This mist won't put people off. If anything, I think it lends a certain spooky ambience to the festival."

Fortunately, his comment about spookiness provided me with an easy in.

"Spooky, yes. I heard there were pirate ghosts at Edward Teach's house last night and that he's gone missing. Does that sort of thing happen very often here?"

Freddie turned around, but continued moving in the same direction, walking backwards so I could see the confused frown on his face.

"The ghosts have struck again?"

Barbie was the first to say, "Again?"

Freddie swung his head her way and broke into a huge smile – Barbie has that effect on men.

"Yes, my beautiful angel. The ghosts of Blackbeard's pirates. Hundreds were hanged when one of Edward Teach's ancestors betrayed them all. This is not the first time their spirits have returned to the island to seek revenge."

"So you believe Edward Teach was targeted by real ghosts?" Jermaine questioned.

Gloria muttered, "I told you they were real."

Freddie stopped just before we reached a line of shops. We were away from the quayside now and reaching the leading edge of the town.

"Welcome to my fine establishment," Freddie raised his arms to either side of his body, drawing our attention to the business to his rear. "Inside you will find the finest souvenirs, postcards, mementos, gifts for your loved ones, and of course the highest quality pirate costumes available on the island."

I doubted we would find anything of quality, but in the two minutes we'd been trailing behind Freddie, I hadn't seen another soul. It was still early, like really early, so businesses were not open yet. I knew it wouldn't take us long to find another place that was open – there had to be restaurants around serving breakfast, but Freddie was right here. He was only interested in selling his wares, but that didn't mean he wasn't filled with answers too.

"The ghosts, Freddie. Tell me about the ghosts, please," I begged.

"Yes, all the finest wares," he replied, backing to his door where he produced a key. "Everything is on sale."

He went inside, the lights flickering to life a moment later.

"Please, Freddie," I called after him. "A friend of ours went missing last night at the same time as Edward. I need to hear what you think you know."

His voice drifted out from inside the shop. "All prices negotiable."

Getting annoyed, I marched up to the door and raised my voice.

"Freddie, I will spend a fortune if you answer my questions."

He started to say something and stopped, his head poking out from behind a rail of pirate clothes to show me where he had gone.

To emphasise my point, I took out my purse, opened it and held up my credit card.

The shopkeeper's eyes were wide with a mix of disbelief and hope.

Barbie went around me, Molly, Jermaine, Gloria, and Hideki all filtering into the shop.

To win the store owner over, Barbie said, "Patty is seriously rich, Freddie. Tell her everything."

We were forming a ring around him, not necessarily trapping him with our bodies, though it could be viewed that way. I preferred to see us as an invested audience. However, if he didn't start telling me something useful soon, I was going to have Jermaine hang him by his ankles.

Pinned in place, offered money, and with both Jermaine and Hideki glaring at him, Freddie finally dropped the salesman of the year act.

"What do you need to know?" he asked.

"I need to know where Edward Teach is. Whoever took him has our friend and I need to get him back." Freddie's brow creased into a frown, and he looked like he wanted to say something. I wasn't finished. "Edward mentioned a local criminal gang or maybe an organisation involved in crime in some way. He was taken before he could tell us who it was. I need to know who that might be and if you don't know, then who would."

Freddie checked to see if I was done firing questions at him.

"I'm confused," he admitted. "You said the ghosts came for him. But now you are asking who has him?"

"Yes, Freddie. The ghosts aren't real." I held my right index finger up at Gloria to keep her from commenting.

"What makes you think that?" Freddie questioned. It was clear from his tone that he believed in the supernatural. "The ghosts of Blackbeard's pirates have visited this island many times in our history. Their attacks have been well documented. They are not the only mysterious threat, of course, we have mermaids who prey on unwary men too. There was an attack just last week, in fact."

"We saw the ghosts," I admitted "We were with Edward when his house was invaded by them. They were no more supernatural than you or I."

"They let you live?" Freddie sounded surprised.

"We ran away," supplied Gloria.

"Screaming," added Molly.

"And trying to not wet our knickers," Gloria felt a need to share.

Dragging Freddie back to where he might provide a useful piece of information, I said, "Never mind the ghosts, Freddie. I believe Edward is being held against his will." I could have added it was that or he was already dead, but if I allowed myself to consider that possibility then it meant Sam was dead too. "Edward mentioned a gang of criminals he believed might be targeting him. This is your town. You say you know everyone. Who was he taking about?"

Freddie gave a hopeless shrug.

"There are undesirable elements here just as there are everywhere else. There are parts of town you don't go to after dark unless you have seedy business interests. I know I said I know everyone, but I don't know people like that."

Unperturbed, I jumped to the next question.

"What about Edward's staff? He employed people at his house, but they all left over the course of the last year or so. The most recent to quit was a woman employed as Edward's housemaid. I'm afraid I don't know her name." My words trailed off; I could see by his eyes that he had an answer lined up.

"I don't know who that might be, but you could talk to Davy."

"Davy?" I repeated the name.

Freddie smiled. "Davy Harris. His family has been on the island since the start. He can trace his roots back to before the Teach family arrived. He worked at the Teach house for about fifty years. I'm not sure when he stopped working there or why, but it wasn't all that long ago. A few months maybe. He'll know who you are looking for."

He might know a lot more than that, I hoped. If he'd worked there for half a century, he could know all manner of dirty secrets about the Teach family.

I posed an obvious question. "Where can I find him?"

11

FISHING FOR BREAKFAST

True to his word, Freddie was knowledgeable about the town and its inhabitants, supplying a full breakdown of where Davy lived and where he was likely to be found at this time of the day plus who he might be with.

Armed with knowledge, it was time to get going, but not before I had made good on my promise to throw down some money. Unfortunately, Freddie's shop was filled with utter garbage. I find these places everywhere I go – shops filled with bric-a-brac and worthless souvenirs, the value of which could only be determined by a person wanting a cheap, plastic fridge magnet, model, or figurine of the place they were currently visiting.

Looking around, I considered just handing Freddie some money and wishing him well – above all else, I didn't have time to dawdle or waste. However, Barbie proposed an idea that made Freddie's day.

"Patty, we might be as well to change our clothes. Everyone we saw yesterday was wearing pirate get up. We stick out in our regular clothes." What she didn't say was that the police might be on the lookout for us – blending in was a sound plan.

"We really do," remarked Hideki, selecting a pirate wench outfit from a rack and holding it up for Barbie to see. The design could only be described as slutty, and he put it back with a snigger when she scowled at him.

Barbie picked out her own outfit, as did the rest of us, each taking a turn in the small changing room Freddie had at the back of the store. Well, the ladies did anyway. Hideki simply stripped off his top half in the shop, exposing his taut midriff and muscular torso. It was gone again a moment later when he donned a deliberately ragged shirt.

Not to be outdone, Jermaine did likewise, but in his case, it exposed the scars he'd accrued in my company. The Godmother's husband had shot him, the bullet leaving a puffy mark of fresh skin that was healed but still very visible. I imagined it would be years before it faded to match the rest of his dark skin.

No one took their time, each of us hustling to change our appearance. Freddie's smile grew even wider when I approached the till, paid for our things, and held up an additional hundred-dollar bill.

"Can we leave our clothes here, please, Freddie?" I asked.

The shopkeeper was only too keen to take my money and give me a reason to return later.

"Bring all your friends next time," he insisted. "Spread the word: Freddie's is the best place for all your needs."

Finally escaping his shop, though we had only been inside for maybe fifteen minutes at most, I was glad to be moving on and strangely discovered I felt more confident now that I was essentially in disguise.

We found Davy Harris exactly where Freddie claimed we would. At this time of the day, he could reliably be found at the eastern end of the docks where he was in the company of three friends: Terrance, Walter, and Horatio. That they were also dressed in pirate garb came as no surprise. They were in their seventies, or maybe just a touch older than that, but appeared fit, healthy, and strong.

Three of them were fishing while the fourth was cooking breakfast over some coals arranged on a foil tray. I saw a line of small fish being barbequed whole, the old man tending them sucking at his fingers when they got too hot.

I didn't know which was which, but only needed to identify which of them was Davy.

"Davy Harris?" Barbie asked with the sort of smile no heterosexual man can resist.

Four sets of eyes swung her way, and a hand went up to reveal which of the men was the one we wanted. He was returning Barbie's smile, but in the manner of a man who was curious about why the drop-dead gorgeous blonde wanted him.

I took over. "Hello," I waved. "I'm Patricia Fisher. I believe you used to work for Edward Teach." It was a statement, not a question. "I'm hoping you can answer a couple of questions. We are in quite dire straits."

Davy turned his head to make eye contact with the man to his left and right. All three had been facing out to sea when we approached them, but were looking our way now. Something passed between the men, an unspoken comment that I hoped someone would explain.

"He owes you money too, does he?" asked Davy, his question accompanied by a weary sigh.

My eyebrows hiked up my head – I hadn't been expecting him to mention money. Grasping his question, I adapted what I was going to say next.

"Is that why you left his employ?"

Davy reeled in his fishing rod, his eyes on the water to make sure it didn't snag on anything. Once he had it under control, he said, "Yes, ma'am. He always had an excuse for why my wages hadn't gone into the bank, but I knew what it was."

"We all did," grumbled the man to his left. His attention was still on the sea and the hope of another bite on his line.

I looked to Davy for clarity.

"Mr Teach … that's the current Mr Teach, not the one I worked for originally, he had ideas about investing in a new enterprise. I don't know much about it, but there were rumours of something big. All his money is tied up in whatever it is."

"Something big?" questioned Molly. "That's about as vague as a person can get."

Davy shrugged. "That's all I know. The rumours were that it was something big, but no one seemed to know what it was."

Gloria challenged him. "Seriously? You were around him all the time, but you don't know what he was trying to invest in?"

Davy frowned, disapproval over being pressed on the accuracy of his statement rising to the surface. "I was the gardener, thank you very much. I spent my time in the gardens."

"They were beautiful," I commented encouragingly, hoping I could keep him on my side because I needed him to tell me more yet. "Do you know the name of a housemaid who used to work at the house too? Edward said she quit just last week."

Bringing his focus back to me, Davy grumbled, "Yes, I know her. You're talking about Mildred. She's my niece's girl. I got her the job there. I still owe her an apology for that. I expect she left for the same reason as me."

"No doubt," echoed the man to his left, teasing his fishing rod and peering into the water.

"Can you tell us where we can find her, please? Or do you have a phone number you can give us? It's really quite urgent?"

Davy's frown remained in place and was joined by three more as all his friends looked our way.

"What is this about?" Davy demanded I reveal a reason for my constant questions. His eyes roved from left to right, checking the faces of the six strangers disturbing his morning fishing expedition.

I saw no reason not to come clean.

"We met Edward Teach last night when we came off the ship." I jerked my head in the direction of the Aurelia which filled the view behind me. "Edward asked for my help and claimed he was worried for his safety. He believed he was being targeted by a local criminal gang and suspected they might use the legend of his family and the ghostly pirates as a cover to do him harm. Before he could explain why, his house was plunged into darkness, and we were attacked."

"By the ghosts of dead pirates!" insisted Gloria, interrupting me unhelpfully.

Her comment caught the old men's attention.

"You saw the ghosts?" questioned the one tending the barbeque, pausing to see what we said and then swearing because his fingers were too close to the heat for too long.

While he sucked on his digits, I replied, "Yes, we did, but I don't believe they were really ghosts."

"That's because you've no imagination, Patricia," snapped Gloria. "Anyone could see they were real."

"They looked real enough to me," agreed Molly.

"They're real, all right," agreed Davy. "I saw them once myself. They were coming out of the surf down by the west pier."

The man to Davy's left chuckled heartily. "That old tale again, Davy? Everyone knows you'd been on the whisky the night before. Why else would you have been sleeping on the beach instead of going home to your wife?"

Davy grumbled, "I saw what I saw."

"Edward went missing and one of our party vanished at the same time. I need to find him. I need your help," I implored. "We've so little to go on, but if Mildred knows anything … anything at all that might help us to find out who took him …"

Davy waved a hand to stop me.

"All right. All right." His right hand was fiddling with a back pocket, a phone appearing in it when it reappeared. "I'll call Mildred and see if she will meet you, but if the ghosts came for Edward and your friend went missing at the same time … they are both in a watery grave."

My breath caught in my throat and my heart gave one big thump. I couldn't bear to think it.

Davy's call connected and he turned away to make his conversation more private. It gave me a few seconds to recover, but the imbalance I felt had not gone unnoticed.

Barbie touched my arm and Jermaine moved in close to my side.

"He's going to be okay, Patty," Barbie assured me. Though she knew no better than me, it was encouraging to hear her say it.

Jermaine added his thoughts. "Samuel is more resilient than

people give him credit for. If he is being held, he will be looking for a way to get free."

"And he'll be trying to rescue Edward at the same time," added Barbie.

They were probably right, but the voice at the back of my head would not shut up. It was an evil voice that wanted to feed me cruel thoughts. It whispered that the 'ghosts' came to the house with criminal intentions, and they would have cared not one jot for the life of a young man caught up in their business. Goodness knows I'd seen enough bodies in the last few months to prove how fleeting life can be.

I began to feel lightheaded once more and had to hold Jermaine's arm for support as I tried to push away the images conjured by my brain.

Davy ended his call and turned to face me. His shoes crunched on the sand coating the seafront, drawing my eyes upward to meet his.

"Mildred wants to meet you. It seems she has something she wants to get off her chest. I told her Mr Teach went missing last night and … well, she may or may not know something. If you find Edward Teach, tell him I want my back pay."

"Where can we find her?" asked Barbie.

12

WHAT MILDRED SAW

Mildred had a new job in the kitchen of a restaurant. This early in the day she hadn't arrived at work yet, but it wasn't her only job and we needed to hustle if we wanted to catch her between them.

Her second job was in a bar at night. You might think that would have ended around midnight and Mildred would be at home in bed as the sun was coming up, but in a town that ran on tourist money, bars stayed open until the last customer left. When Davy called her, she was just on her way home to eat and get a quick nap.

"I could do with one of them rickshaw things again," announced Gloria. "My hip is giving me gyp."

In her eighties, Gloria was quite sprightly, but a mode of transport that would limit the time she spent on her feet was a good idea.

Jermaine sucked some air between his teeth. "I'm not sure they operate this early in the day, Mrs Chalk."

We were heading back into the town centre from the beach where we met Davy. Mildred had agreed to meet us where the town's main thoroughfare met the docks. It was an indirect route for her according to Davy, an extra mile to walk on tired legs, which just went to show how keen she was to talk to someone.

There were no rickshaws that we could see, not that we could see more than a few yards in the thick fog. Where last night there had been crowds of revellers in their pirate costumes and passengers from the ship pouring out to fill the streets, now the town felt empty.

The fog clung to our clothing, dampening it. After some time, the moisture would soak through, but it was still warm out and I expected the heat of the sun this close to the equator would burn off the fog as the day wore on.

Every now and then we would see someone moving in the fog. Or rather, I thought I did, but each swirl of mist with a shadow moving through would be eaten up before I had a chance to focus my eyes.

The towering form of the Aurelia dominated everything to our left as we made our way back along the sea front. Lights in the cabins and on the decks made it easier to see, but even then it was no more than a dark blob with some patches of distorted light.

When we reached the right place, I was disappointed to not find Mildred waiting for us, but it turned out I was wrong, and we just couldn't see her.

A voice from our left said, "Hello? Are you looking for me?"

As one, we all turned to find a small woman in her mid-twenties stepping out from under the awning of a shop. Dressed to show off as much skin as possible, I silently questioned what sort of bar she worked in. She looked tired and wore tatty running shoes on her feet that did not go with her outfit and had undoubtedly replaced a pair of heels the moment her shift ended.

Closest to her, Hideki asked, "Mildred?"

She came closer, the hazy effect of the fog fading when she got to within a couple of yards. We gathered in a group around her.

"Hello, Mildred. I'm Patricia Fisher." I made sure I had her attention, then jumped in with a question, wasting no time. "Are you aware that Edward Teach went missing last night?"

She nodded that she did, once again showing how tired she was by the lack of effort behind it.

"Lots of people are talking about it. Did someone else go missing too? Have I got that right?"

Gloria butted in, "People are talking about it? What are they saying? What people are we talking about? It's my grandson who went missing along with that Mr Teach. Where will the ghosts take him, do you know?"

Bombarded with questions, Mildred's eyes flitted from me to Gloria and back again.

"I, ah …"

Placing a hand on Gloria's arm – it was concern for Sam that drove her to be involved and I understood her thirst to find answers – I brought Mildred's attention back to me.

"Yes, Mildred, one of our friends went missing. Anything you can tell us will be enormously helpful."

To my surprise, the young woman snorted a laugh, and I might have questioned why if she hadn't then said, "I can do better than that. I can tell you who took them."

We all held our collective breath, waiting for her to tell us the name.

Before we needed to prompt her, she looked about, clearly checking to see if there was anyone within earshot other than my friends. Looking nervous, she leaned in close to me and whispered, "Tommy DeMeco."

Barbie was instantly on her phone, her thumbs flashing about the screen as she looked up who that was.

I went for the direct approach.

"Who is Tommy DeM …"

The moment I said his name, Mildred started shushing me and flapping her arms to make me stop talking.

"Shhhhh! Someone will hear! He's a bad man, that's who he is. If he so much as hears a rumour that I was saying his name in public …" She didn't feel a need to finish her sentence, or perhaps just didn't wish to articulate the events that could follow.

Dropping my voice to a whisper, I asked, "Okay. Don't worry, I'll be discreet. I need to know what you know though, Mildred. Why would he take Edward and Sam?"

Mildred, tired though she clearly was, became animated when she started to tell us about recent events at Edward's house and why she had chosen to leave his employment. She admitted that getting paid had become a little sporadic in recent months, confirming to some extent the report we got from Davy Harris, but it was everything else she told us that held our interest.

We had moved out of the street and under the awning where she had been waiting for us. The town was beginning to wake up, street traders arriving to hawk their wares to the thousands of tourists who would soon begin to leave the ship. I heard the clopping sound of horse hooves through the mist and remembered the excursion we were supposed to be taking later today. I had forgotten to cancel our booking.

If we found Sam in the next hour, we could still fit it in, but I doubted anyone in my team would want to. It was insignificant.

"Mr Teach was worried about something," Mildred revealed, though we already knew that snippet of detail – that he'd hired us was proof enough. "I heard him shouting on the phone a few times, and he would use the most awful language."

"Do you know who he was talking to? Or what it was about?" I pressed her.

Mildred shook her head. "Sorry, no. I made a point of not being nosey; that would be a good way to lose a job. If I heard him on the phone, I went the other way. It was a big house, there was always somewhere else I could be cleaning."

I was letting her talk and trying to keep my desperate need to get to the point in check. I wanted to know where to find Tommy DeMeco and what particular beef he had with Edward that had caused him to attack his house and take him last night. Maybe I couldn't help Edward. Maybe he had made his own bed and was now going to have to lie in it. Whatever their quarrel, it had nothing to do with Sam. Tommy DeMeco was a criminal and I believed it would be possible to leverage him. If he wanted money, I would buy Sam back.

Whatever it took.

Finally, after I had confirmed Mildred knew almost nothing about her former boss's business dealings, she got to the bit about Tommy DeMeco. I had already established she didn't know whether

Edward was talking to him on the phone or not, but she did have reason to believe they were connected somehow.

"He came to the house," Mildred told us. She was wringing her hands and still looking around nervously while she talked. "I quit the same day. Or rather, I just never showed up for work again. My uncle had been telling me to do so for ages, but Mr Teach had always been good with the wages until a few months ago. I figured he would get things back on track and I wanted the money that was already owed to me. I have rent to pay and …"

Her personal problems were all very interesting, and I had no wish to be rude, but time was ticking by, and her rent wasn't going to get Sam back.

"Tommy DeMeco, Mildred," I cut over her to bring her focus back. "Why was he at Edward's house? What did he want?"

Unhappy that I had cut her off when she was lamenting her problems, I got a frown and a curt response.

"I have no idea. I told you already, I don't like to be nosey."

"I'm sorry," I apologised and saw her recognise the anguish in my face. It had the desired effect, cooling her off again.

"The moment I saw Tommy DeMeco arrive, I grabbed my things and went out the back. I know two of his goons and they know me. I don't need any trouble from them."

"Know them how?" asked Barbie, picking up on Mildred's tone.

Scrunching up her face as if there was something distasteful in her mouth, Mildred wrestled with how to answer.

"I dated them," she admitted after a second of pause.

Gloria repeated, "Them?"

"Not at the same time," frowned Mildred. "I worked as a dancer in Tommy's nightclub for a time and … well, I guess I got a lot of attention."

I could see it happening. Mildred was an attractive young woman.

"So you left the house when you saw Tommy DeMeco arrive with his men," I confirmed. "How many men?"

Mildred shrugged one shoulder. "Ten? A dozen? He never goes anywhere without an entourage, and they are always armed. Look,

I'm sorry, but I don't know what he might have wanted with Mr Teach. I can only guess that it was something bad though – Tommy DeMeco doesn't have any other kind of business to conduct."

This was not welcome news, but we were making progress. Tommy DeMeco was the local gang boss Edward mentioned but never got to name, I was almost certain of it. In all likelihood Edward had gotten himself mixed up in something unsavoury and it had backfired on him. Was he trying to hire Tommy and his men to do something illegal? He was involved in something big if Davy had it right.

All I had were questions and loose ends, but I wasn't trying to solve a mystery, I just wanted to get Sam back. If Tommy had him, then I was going to see him next.

I asked the question I wanted an answer to more than any other.

13

STRAWBERRY MOONS

I called Alistair on our way to Tommy DeMeco's nightclub. According to Mildred that was where we would find him at this time of day. Really, I didn't need to know anything else. His business with Edward could stay private; I didn't have to care what he was doing at Edward's house a week ago. I just needed to know where to find him and then figure out how to get the local criminal to admit that he had Sam.

"Patricia," Alistair answered, "how are you getting along? We think we have a lead."

This came as surprising news to me. "Really? What is it?"

Alistair's voice became muffled, his hand over the mouthpiece so he could say something to someone else. I caught Martin's voice replying when Alistair removed his hand.

"Sorry, darling, we are just arriving. Can I call you back?"

"Where?" I demanded. "Where are you arriving?"

"Oh," he said, sensing that he needed to tell me a little more than 'he'd found a lead'. "A few miles away around to the west from Torruga. There's an old woman here who used to work for the Teach family. We met her grandson, and he claims she knows all manner of dark family secrets. Like I said, we are just arriving, so we'll know more shortly, I hope. How are you getting on?"

I opened my mouth to tell him about Tommy DeMeco, but stopped myself. Telling Alistair I was planning to walk into the premises of a known hoodlum was not going to do me any favours. For a start he would beg me to wait and then rush to get to my location with his half of the team.

The whole point of splitting up was to cover more ground. He had a lead and I needed to let him follow it up.

Choosing my words so they would be truthful, I said, "Nothing so far. I'll let you know if anything develops."

He wished me luck, expressed his love, and ended the call.

Barbie was grinning at me when I put my phone away and looked in her direction.

"You were lying through your teeth, Patricia Fisher."

"Is it much farther?" asked Gloria, sucking air between her teeth and putting her hands on her hips as she took a breather.

The dominant feature of Torruga from a geological perspective is the gradient on which it is built. From the sea it tapers gently inward for a distance of about two hundred yards, gaining perhaps no more than a couple of yards in height. Then the gradient increases sharply, the gradient becoming a slope and then a hill as the land climbed toward the mountains behind it.

I was perspiring, and I was beginning to regret my pirate outfit. The dress was a bit too baggy, and the boots were cheap and thus not the best thing to be walking long distances in. I'd kept my bra on – heaven knows I wasn't taking that off as Barbie had hers because it didn't go with the outfit she'd chosen - but had to keep tugging at the top of the dress every few yards to keep it in place.

It was a mercy then when we heard a rickshaw coming out of the murky mist, the sound of its wheels slowly rotating a dead giveaway.

Gloria was the first to respond.

"Oi, over here!" she shouted. "Rickshaw for one!"

Jermaine moved to intercept it, aiming to head it off.

A man holding a handle in each hand coasted into view, the fog seemingly regurgitating him, and Gloria said some rude words.

It wasn't a rickshaw at all, but a man on his way to the docks with his wares on a hand cart. He passed us by with a bemused expression, undoubtedly wondering where we were going so far from the docks at this time of the morning.

Gloria continued to moan and mutter, complaining about her hip and her feet and the bunion on her big toe until twenty minutes later we arrived at Strawberry Moons Nightclub. Finding it had been easy enough even if it was all uphill to get there. I had to wonder if the islanders were all long lived because they had to walk everywhere.

The limited area of the town, hemmed in by sea and mountains, meant there was little space between any of the buildings. We had just passed through a residential area – houses with small gardens – and were now looking at a row of industrial units. The nightclub was just one of them.

I spotted a lamppost and crossed to it, using its solidity to keep myself upright while I caught my breath. Looking around, Hideki, Jermaine, Molly and most especially Barbie all looked fresh and untroubled by the exertion required to reach our destination. Apart from a few beads of perspiration in deference to the warmth, held extra close by the mist, they could have just stepped off the ship.

Barbie came over to check on me. "You doing okay there, Patty?"

I gave her a thumbs up and pushed off the lamppost. Sucking in a deep lungful of air, I said, "No time to be anything else. Sam could be in this building," I remarked as we all stared at the two story, gaudy nightclub. The neon lights were off, and it was quiet, but litter and mess from the previous evening's debauchery were evident all around it. Whoever had come here to party last night had enjoyed a wild time.

There was nothing behind the nightclub – it sat right at the edge of the town where the gradient became too steep for people to build on. Gaps ran between the nightclub and the buildings to its left and right providing access to the rear. The front entrance where customers would be greeted was clearly locked; a chain looped through the door handles making entry that way unlikely. So around the back we went.

No one said it, but we were looking for a way to break in. We were uninvited and though we could find a door and hammer on it, sneaking in and finding Sam before they even knew we were there sounded like a better plan.

"Cooeee!" called Gloria, putting her face up to a window that was open a crack. "Anyone in there? I'd like my grandson back, please."

In the silence that pervaded at this end of the town, her shout would have woken the dead. We all froze, each saying a silent prayer that the people inside had somehow not heard her.

I counted to three and was about to breathe a sigh of relief when Gloria's call was answered by the sound of running feet echoing out from inside. The feet were accompanied by raised voices as someone barked orders and others responded.

Barbie gripped my arm. "Patty? Should we run?"

Molly muttered, "I'm beginning to doubt the reward money for this case is worth it."

In different circumstances, I would be leaving my athletic friend in my dust. Today, I chose to stand my ground. The element of surprise might be lost, but I needed to meet Tommy DeMeco and that seemed likely to happen now.

A door to our left burst open and the sound of another one around the corner to our right effectively pinned the six of us in place. Our backs were quite literally to the wall, although in today's case it was a mountain. With nowhere to go and heavyset men approaching us from both sides, we gathered into a tight ball.

These were the first people I had seen on the island who were not dressed as pirates. Ironic really considering I was certain these were the ones who invaded Edward's home last night dressed as the ghosts.

I felt Jermaine's hand brush lightly against my shoulder and his deep bass voice appeared next to my ear.

"Say the word and I will disable them, madam. They do not

appear to be armed." His voice was a whisper Tommy DeMeco's men couldn't hear, but I replied with a small shake of my head.

We were badly outnumbered – twelve of them to only six of us and our number included me, whose fighting technique was to scream and hope I didn't wet myself, and Gloria who was in her eighties. I had insisted she leave her house brick behind and now found myself ruing that decision.

"We are here to see Tommy DeMeco," I announced loudly and with far more confidence than I felt.

A spokesperson, undoubtedly a loyal lieutenant of the boss, answered.

"Tourists?" he identified what we were with a frown. Using one hand to tell the men on both sides of my group to stand down, he added, "The cheap costumes are a dead giveaway. Fresh off the boat. You have no business with Mr DeMeco. Please enjoy the time you have here and come back tonight when we are open."

Jermaine was right that they were not armed, but only in the sense that they didn't appear to be carrying guns. They had bats and hook-ended steel bars instead. They were professional criminals – trust me I've met enough to know what I am looking at – but they were offering us the chance to leave.

If only that were an option I could take.

"I need to speak with Tommy DeMeco," I stated again, surprising the spokesperson who had expected us to walk away. When he gave me a questioning look, I said, "I know about his business with Edward Teach."

The second the words left my mouth I could see it had been the wrong thing to say. The weapons, which most of the men carrying them had been trying to hide, placing their hands behind their backs or otherwise moving them out of sight like a naughty child holding the evidence of his or her wrongdoing, were suddenly very much visible again.

The spokesperson snorted a dry laugh. "Lady. You're in big trouble." To the men around him, he said, "Get them inside."

Next to me, Jermaine tensed, and I saw Hideki do the same. They were both accomplished martial artists and serious individuals.

I didn't want to be protected though, I wanted to get inside so I could talk to Tommy DeMeco.

In response to Jermaine and Hideki, and to Molly and Barbie too who both looked ready to fight if less than thrilled at the prospect, the men surrounding us all fell into battle stances.

Taking Jermaine's hand and interlocking his fingers with mine, I smiled up at him.

"Let them lead us to where we want to go."

Tommy DeMeco's men heard me, their reactions a mix of disbelief and mild amusement.

The spokesperson shook his head and laughed.

"Lady, you are one crazy broad." Talking to his colleagues, he said, "She wants to see Tommy DeMeco. Sure, just show up at his place and accuse him of illegal activity. That ought to do it."

His comments were met with a chorus of laughter as he led the way back into the building. Silently I noted that I hadn't mentioned anything illegal.

I'd said business with Edward. I had no idea what it could be, but now I knew it was something that broke the law.

It was darker inside than it was out, but not by much. Kept at bay by the fog, the morning sun might have risen, but the island was suspended in an almost crack-of-dawn like etherealness. When a light came on above my head, the change in brightness stung my eyes. I was still blinking when we passed through a doorway and out of the corridor.

Arriving in a passageway that ran crossways to the previous one, we turned left but did not go far.

The spokesman had led the way until now, but ahead of us was another man, this one wearing a suit. He was taller and broader than Jermaine and had the same clinical eyes, assessing all he saw and judging what threat it might hold. His head was enormous, the forehead sloping down to a set of heavy eyebrows. With his short, buzz cut black hair, he looked like a white gorilla.

"You were told to get rid of them," rumbled the gorilla in the suit. His voice was so deep it sounded like it emanated from beneath his feet. Somewhere in hell possibly.

Spokesman shrugged his shoulders in an exaggerated way and went right up to the gorilla, leaning in so he could speak at a non-audible volume.

We all saw it when he got to the good bit and the gorilla's disinterest abruptly shifted. His eyes flicked up and a hand swung backward to knock on the door he protected.

"What?" called a voice from within. "I'm busy."

"Got a problem, boss," grumbled the gorilla.

His announcement was met with cursing, mostly about having to do everything himself and why it was that he employed such incompetents.

The rightmost of a pair of double doors shot inward with an angry jerk, and Tommy DeMeco walked out. I mean, I figured it had to be him. Who else could it be?

"Mr DeMeco?" I addressed him directly, cutting over his conversation.

A mumbling sound came from somewhere in the room. To my ears it sounded like someone trying to speak around a gag and I almost started running when the thought that it might be Sam flooded my brain.

The man who had launched himself so angrily from the room was now standing in the corridor. Unlike his gorilla, he was not wearing a suit. He had on a pair of baggy shorts and a vest. A basketball outfit, my brain supplied. To complete the look, his feet bore those oversized sports shoes that come up around the ankle and a pair of white tube socks that ended halfway up his shins.

I thought he looked ridiculous, most especially since he was a skinny whelp of a man, but I doubted saying so would do me any favours.

The gorilla whispered in his boss's ear much as the spokesman had whispered in his. The same eye flare of surprise came and the oddly dressed man turned to face me.

I got to see the smear of blood on the front of his baggy vest, and I lost my cool.

"Is that Sam's blood?" I raged. "Did you hurt him?" I started to move, setting off to see who it was I could still hear groaning out of sight in the room the gang boss had just left. I couldn't say what I was thinking, or even that I was. Chances were I was going to whack the skinny basketball fan on the head if he got in my way.

It was a mercy then that I only got to take one pace before Jermaine grabbed my arm and half a dozen of the goons we met outside stepped in to block my path.

"Well, well," said Tommy DeMeco in a horrible cockney accent that seemed completely out of place in this paradise island. "What have we here? My boys tell me you think you know something about Edward Teach. Maybe you should tell me everything you know. If I like what I hear, I might not cut all of you into little pieces …" He stopped speaking, but didn't alter his gaze, his eyes boring into mine. He wasn't finished talking though and he added, "… only some of you."

"Only some of us what?" questioned Gloria. "Can you speak up, please?"

Barbie's fingers found mine, taking my hand so she had someone to hold on to. Not for the first time I wondered how it was that our little break ashore had gone so horribly wrong.

"Sam," I blurted. "I just want Sam. I can pay you for him. Is he hurt?" I was both filled with rage and completely terrified at the same time. We had been in bad situations before, and this was right up there with them.

Tommy folded his arms and looked me up and down in a manner that suggested he was assessing me.

"How much?"

"For Sam? I need to see him," I replied, hope blooming in my chest. If Tommy DeMeco was prepared to negotiate, we were in business. I would feel bad because it would be the Maharaja's money I was spending, but I would do it anyway.

"We'll get to that once we've agreed a price. I'm a man of refined tastes," he jabbered, his accent making him sound anything but. "Also," he added when a new thought crossed his mind. "I want to know what you know about Edward Teach. My boys tell me you know about our business. Why don't you tell me what you know?"

His sentence was posed as a polite invitation, but I knew it was anything but.

Gloria interrupted again. "Have you got my grandson or not, you horrible little twerp?"

Tommy DeMeco's features darkened instantly.

"You think you can speak to me like that and get away with it, old lady?"

"I don't see why not," Gloria cackled. "I'm too old to be scared by a man dressed in his daddy's shorts."

Her comment ought not to have been funny to any of us, but Molly snorted a laugh she just couldn't keep inside, and she wasn't alone. Some of Tommy's men had to fight hard to keep the smiles from their faces and all because Gloria had hit the nail on its head.

Tommy DeMeco did look like he's borrowed his father's clothes. The bagginess of the basketball shorts made them look ten sizes too big for his skinny frame.

The gang boss's cheeks twitched with rage.

"If you hurt us, you won't get a penny," I flung the words from my mouth as if they could act as a defensive barrier. From the corner of my mouth, I hissed, "Gloria, please stop provoking him!"

Gloria began muttering as I shot Tommy DeMeco an imploring look.

"Please. I just want Sam back. My name is Patricia Fisher. I'm friends with the Maharaja of Zangrabar. He's the third richest man on the planet …"

Spokesman clicked his fingers and pointed at me, a big beaming smile on his face when he boomed, "Granny Pants!" Taking his eyes off me for a scant moment, he remarked to his boss, "Remember that picture I showed you? The woman who fell off the stage at that Maharaja's big ceremony thing. She showed the world her big butt. It's the same woman!" he announced triumphantly.

Tommy DeMeco couldn't care less. "Shut up, Danny."

Spokesman – I kept calling him that in my head because I preferred it to Danny – clamped his lips together.

"A hundred million dollars, US," said Tommy, advancing toward me. "If you're that stinking rich, I want a hundred million."

Now my brain was working overtime. There was no way in hell I could give Tommy anywhere near that kind of money. I had thought I might swing a hundred thousand or maybe even a couple of hundred thousand, but he was asking for nine figures like it was something that could happen.

I couldn't tell him that though, I had to figure out how to get Sam back first.

"That's going to take a while," I replied in an apologetic tone.

The muffled groaning sound of pain coming from inside DeMeco's office hadn't let up the whole time we'd been talking. I still didn't know if it was Sam in there or not, but I needed to find out.

"Can we see him," I begged. "I need to know that he's okay."

Unable to keep her mouth shut, Gloria started again.

"You're not getting a penny until you show me my grandson."

It proved too much for our host this time.

Tommy sneered in a most unpleasant manner, "You know what? I'm going about this all wrong. There are six of you. I think maybe that's too many. I want to know what you know about my business with Edward Teach and when I start killing your friends, you're going to tell me everything you know."

Like a silent message had been passed, all the thugs in the corridor immediately lifted their bats and blades or whatever they held.

There was whispering coming from my friends. I think Barbie tried to tell me something, but the blood thundering through my head made it so I couldn't hear her words.

"I'll tell you everything now," I blurted the words, panic taking over my mouth. "We heard you were at his house a week ago. That's all. I'm just guessing the rest." I couldn't mention Mildred and that she had assured us Tommy DeMeco was behind Edward's disappearance. "I don't know what it's all about and I don't care. I just want Sam back!"

Ignoring me completely, Tommy nodded his head at Spokesman. "Bring me the old bag. We'll start with her."

"I'm telling you the truth!" I wailed, unable to believe this was happening. "We don't know anything!"

"Old bag?" questioned Gloria.

The whispering in my group stopped.

As ordered, Danny the spokesman closed the short distance between us and held out his hand expecting Gloria to comply and take it.

When she did, my eyes bugged out of my head.

"Gloria, no!" I screeched, terrified about what might be about to happen.

Spokesman's head twitched in my direction, a leering smile on his face and a smart remark on his lips. Whatever it was he planned to say stayed with him forever though for Gloria swung her handbag upward from the floor to connect between his unsuspecting legs.

When it struck home, she yelled, "God be with you!"

Jermaine and Hideki chose that moment to launch an attack they had clearly been planning. Caught in the middle of it, I squealed in fright and did my utmost to not have a heart attack.

We were in a tight corridor no more than a yard and a half across and there were ten or more men with weapons on either side of us. It ought to have put us at an enormous disadvantage, but instead, the confined space meant only two or at best three of Tommy's men could attack at once.

You might think that would easily be enough, but that's because you haven't seen Jermaine in action. Arms and legs whirled, scything into body parts with a crunching efficiency that ensured whatever he hit stayed that way. As each man fell to the floor, those trying to fight found themselves attempting to overcome a trip hazard in addition to the muscular Jamaican ninja attempting to take their heads off.

Between our position and where Tommy DeMeco stood with his gorilla, it was Hideki handing out the pain. Smaller and more compact than Jermaine, he was also faster. I squealed in fright when someone swung a two-foot-long blade at his head, but it passed through empty air, Hideki having already moved.

The machete wielding man's feet were chopped out from beneath him as Hideki spun and leapt, an arcing leg swinging down to strike the man's skull with a heel.

This all happened in the five seconds that followed Gloria swinging her handbag and I was still waiting to see if my heart was going to bother beating again.

"God be with you!" yelled Gloria again, swinging her handbag downward to crunch into the head of a man Hideki had just felled.

Unable to convince my own body to move, the terror of watching my friends fight for their lives enough to petrify me, my heart suddenly began to thump again when I spotted Gorilla reaching inside his jacket.

I knew he was going to produce a gun, but could not shout a warning fast enough.

"Patty, duck!" yelled Barbie, scaring me once again. I didn't get the chance to duck, I just got slammed out of the way when my blonde friend shoved by me.

Resourceful, and devious enough to have broken the rules, both Barbie and Molly had produced taser guns. The security team on the ship carry them at all times but are not allowed to take them ashore.

I wasn't going to tell anyone.

They both fired at the same time, their electrodes hitting Gorilla in his upper chest just as his hand was clearing his jacket. He twitched, spasming in place for two seconds before falling over backwards.

Tommy DeMeco's eyes were bugging from his head.

"Madam, we must depart," called out Jermaine. Even in a situation such as this one, he was able to remain calm and butlerlike.

More than half the thugs were down, and the rest were running away. I thought for a moment that we had won, but I heard departing voices yelling about getting their guns.

"Now you're gonna pay," raged DeMeco, running into his office and slamming the door shut before Hideki or Barbie could get to him.

Barbie screamed her frustration and tore at the door handle.

"Ooh, I need a lie down," groaned Gloria, leaning against the wall. "And maybe a nice cup of tea. With a shot or two of whisky in it."

Gasping a breath, Molly asked, "What was with all that 'God be with you' stuff?"

Gloria sniggered, reaching into her handbag to show off the thick hardback Bible she had inside it. I might have forced her to give up the house brick, but she wasn't defeated that easily.

"Are the doors locked?" I shouted, my question aimed at Barbie who nodded her head before throwing her shoulder at them.

"Madam?" Jermaine called to get my attention. "I fear we really must take this opportunity to escape the premises."

"Not without Sam," I insisted, unable to take my eyes off Barbie. The doors were rattling every time she hit them, and Hideki was running to lend his weight.

Molly joined him too, and when I started in their direction, Jermaine raced by me to get there first. We could hear Tommy DeMeco's men returning and I knew we had probably already missed our chance to vanish into the fog outside. It was too late to do anything about that now, but perhaps we could trap Tommy in his office and call the police to our location. If we had Sam back and his kidnapper in custody, how could they not come?

Barbie shouted a count down from three and five of us slammed our bodies into the double doors. They folded inward at the middle, opening to spill us into the unknown room that lay beyond.

I stumbled and almost fell, staying upright only because Jermaine caught me. Even out of control my eyes had been searching the room for my young assistant.

Tommy DeMeco, without his goons to protect him, looked terrified. He held a bat in his hands, high up by his head like he was waiting for a pitch. Jermaine and Hideki had taken a moment to assess the threat he represented and dismissed him, reversing their course to get the doors shut again.

There was no sign of Sam at all, but no sooner had a fresh band of worry started to constrict my chest, than I heard the muffled voice coming from behind a desk. Tommy was standing in front of it, the bat held like a threat, not that anyone seemed particularly concerned about it.

"Sam!" I cried, getting an urgent muffled response from behind the desk.

From behind me, Hideki said, "These doors are broken. We're going to have to barricade them."

Tommy sneered, "There's no way out of here. You're trapped. Now, tell me what you did with Edward Teach and maybe I'll leave some of you with the ability to walk."

Barbie advanced on him, determined strides never wavering as she closed the gap between them.

Tommy twitched his arms, trying to feign his swing and cause her to duck. Barbie's step didn't so much as slow, and I found out why a second later. She was the decoy. With all his attention on her, Tommy DeMeco didn't see Molly throw a four-hole punch at his head. The heavy item of office equipment clattered into the side of his skull, drawing a yowl of pain that made him drop his bat to grab his head.

Barbie grabbed his head too, clamping her hands over his to pin them in place. This was not the first time I had seen my beautiful friend's face contorted with anger, but it came as a shock just the same. Her perfect features were ugly for a second as rage took over, but we were in a fight for our lives it seemed, and we were finally about to rescue Sam.

With a yank, Barbie swivelled off a back foot and threw Tommy DeMeco across the room. He hit the floor with his shoulder, rolling and sprawling, but whether he got up or not I could not tell because I was running to get to Sam. My head and heart were filled with prayers that he might be relatively unharmed despite the blood on Tommy's vest.

Barbie got their first, going over the desk as I was rounding it, but we both saw it at the same time.

14

PETER WEBSTER

It wasn't Sam.

I gasped, shock and horror sucking the oxygen from my brain. There was a man behind the desk, but it wasn't my assistant. The bound and gagged form staring up at me with hopeful eyes was a balding, tubby guy in his forties.

The blood on Tommy's basketball shirt had to have come from whoever the man on the floor was. His nose appeared to be broken, but other than that, he looked to be unharmed. He was terrified though and very clear about his request to be untied.

Tommy DeMeco's men were arriving outside his office; their shouts and curses loud enough to drown out our voices unless we shouted. They were going to come through the doors and there was little we could do to stop them.

Or so I thought.

While Barbie and I worked on the bindings of the man we'd found, Jermaine stalked across the room to grab the crime boss. Tommy tried to swat my butler's hands away, but it was like watching a small child battle an adult. When Tommy made himself heavy, Jermaine simply hoisted him into the air.

Jermaine and Hideki had piled a few pieces of furniture in front of the double doors. It had bought some time because the men outside couldn't just kick the doors open, but it wouldn't hold them for long and I could hear them cocking their guns.

"You're all going to die now," taunted Tommy, flailing at Jermaine's arms still. "They are going to fill this room with bullets when I tell them to."

Jermaine lifted the crime boss up and onto the pile of furniture, pushing him up against the double doors so his face and chest were flat against them.

"Golly, Sir. Are you sure that's a good idea?" he asked.

With a wail of fright, Tommy screamed, "Nobody shoot! You hear me? If you shoot, you'll hit me. Just wait, okay?"

Barbie got the gag undone, finally freeing the man we'd found so he could speak.

"Thank you! Goodness, thank you so much! I thought they were going to kill me," he rattled off sentences in a staccato burst of words.

I was still working on the cords around his feet and really needed a knife to cut through them.

"Who are you?" I begged to know. "Do you know Edward Teach? Have you seen him here in the last few hours? Or another man, a younger man in his early thirties with Downs syndrome."

Jermaine called out, "Madam, we need to think about leaving. Might I make a proposal?"

Barbie shouted, "Stop being calm, you idiot! Panic and sweat like the rest of us, won't you?"

Gloria asked, "Is there anything to drink? I'm feeling a little parched. I don't want much. Just a little pick me up."

A bullet shot through the door three inches from Tommy DeMeco's head and caused a fresh torrent of unprintable words to gush from his lips. It bought us a moment of respite if nothing else as the men outside stopped trying to break in and fell to arguing about what to do next.

"Your name?" I repeated my question to the man on the carpet as I finally worked the knot around his ankles loose.

"Peter. Peter Webster. They grabbed me when I was on my way

home from work last night. I got stuffed into a trunk and loaded onto a cart. They told me to keep quiet or they would cut off my toes, so I did."

"Why did they grab you?" I begged to know, hoping it might have something to do with Edward's disappearance and why Tommy DeMeco was after him.

Peter blurted, "I'm just an accountant. I don't know anything. I don't have any power." It struck me as an odd answer to give to my question, but further cross-examination was going to have to wait.

Barbie got his hands free, and the man was able to get up. He immediately felt his nose.

"Is it broken?" he asked, touching it carefully and wincing when he did.

I nodded. "Most likely, yes." I had all manner of questions to ask about why he was being tortured by Tommy DeMeco, but the gang boss spoke first.

"I'm not finished with you, Webster. I want my money. I don't care who has it. If I don't get it back, I'll hunt you down like the dog you are."

Jermaine, one hand gripping the back of Tommy's basketball vest pulled him away from the door to then slam him back into it.

"Please refrain from speaking unless invited to do so, Sir."

Barbie bounced up and onto her feet. "We need a way out," she stated the obvious. Unfortunately, what she didn't have to say was that there were no windows, and the only doors were the ones Tommy DeMeco was currently pressed against.

Once again, Jermaine said, "I believe I may have a solution, madam."

Pulling Peter Webster off the carpet and onto his feet, I implored Jermaine, "Whatever you have planned, please just do it, sweetie. I don't feel this is the right time for a debate."

Tommy laughed, "There is no other way out, you idiots. Surrender now and I will be lenient."

I didn't believe him for a second.

Jermaine switched places with Hideki, and Molly jumped in to help hold the struggling crime lord in place. I watched with confusion as my butler went to a wall to my left and started to hump a filing cabinet out of the way.

Hoping he had some genius plan up his sleeve, I still couldn't leave if Sam was here. To Peter Webster, I repeated the question about my missing assistant.

"A kid with Downs?" Peter shook his head. "No, I haven't seen anyone here except the hoods who grabbed me this morning."

I voiced my frustration, snarling in despair like a caged animal.

"Did you ever have Sam and Edward?" I roared at Tommy. I came up next to the doors so I could see his face as it was pressed against the wood. "Did you?"

The skinny wretch grinned at me and laughed. "I have no idea what you are talking about, woman."

Behind me, what sounded like a fist going through a wall turned out to be precisely that. I twisted around to find Jermaine pulling his arm back out through the hole he'd just made.

Barbie gawped. "It's a stud wall," she remarked, rushing to Jermaine's side so she too could rip at the plasterboard. In seconds they were through the first layer and ready to break through the thin wall on the other side.

"I noticed the join in the boards, madam," Jermaine explained. "I believe, if we are lucky, we will break through well away from the men gathered outside the doors."

Tommy sucked in a deep breath to shout out our plan, but the words never left his mouth. Hideki gripped his neck, applying a sleeper hold with one hand. The mob boss went limp, falling back into Hideki's arms.

"We're escaping?" asked Peter.

Gloria, who had found herself a chair to sit in, levered herself out of it. Molly ran to her side to give her a hand.

Hideki asked, "What do I do with him?" He had hold of Tommy's vest by the neck.

I needed only a second to consider my answer. "Bring him. I still have questions, and they might not shoot if we have their boss."

Barbie and Jermaine took two steps back, then ran at the plasterboard, blasting their way through it in one go. Fine white particles of plaster filled the air, but we had an exit, and it was clear DeMeco's men didn't know about it.

To buy a few extra seconds, I shouted to the men outside Tommy's office, "We're coming out, okay? We surrender. Just give us a minute to clear away the barricade."

A few fresh curses came my way, mostly telling me to move faster, but they faded behind me as I ducked through the new hole in the back of the office.

It led into a new corridor; one we hadn't been in before. We could hear Tommy's men, the voices echoing through the building, but keeping quiet, we snuck away.

At a junction, Barbie and Jermaine paused. Which way might lead us out? There was no need to articulate their question as they peered left and right, but the answer came from an unexpected source.

"Go right," hissed Peter. "There're no exits on this floor without going back past his men, but if we go up the stairs there is a fire exit and a ladder leading down."

We didn't question him, especially since we could hear that Tommy's men had grown impatient and were once again trying to force their way into the office. The stairs were right around the corner proving Peter knew where he was going, and the fire exit was right there when we got to the next floor.

"Will it set off an alarm?" Barbie hissed before she pushed the door open.

Peter didn't know the answer to that question, but when Barbie shoved it open and the swirling fog outside poured in, no wailing siren filled the air.

We were in the space between buildings and the route to safety lay to our right. Barbie swung out and started down the ladder, Molly hot on her heels.

"Can you manage?" I asked Gloria.

She pulled a face and said, "It's been a while since I scaled a ladder, dearie, but I think I'll manage." Her reply carried the tone of a person who was being underestimated. I'd worried she might be feeling frail, but she was ready for anything and displeased to have had her capability to keep up questioned.

As she descended, I turned to Hideki. "Can you climb down with him on your shoulders?"

Hideki shrugged. "Maybe. But I wasn't planning to." Before I could question what he meant, Hideki leaned to one side and let Tommy fall, calling, "Watch out below," to Barbie who had to sidestep the falling gangster.

Tommy crashed to the ground feet first and kind of splodged into a floppy mess at Barbie's feet. Molly took great pleasure in stepping onto him as she came off the ladder.

With everyone on the ground, we wasted no time getting to the leading edge of the building. The fog was as thick as ever, the visibility no greater than a few yards. However, what before had been a problem now worked in our favour.

We checked to see if the coast was clear, but all we could really do was listen. With no indication that Tommy's men knew we had escaped, we got moving. Navigating in the pea soup weather was easy enough – we just pointed our feet down the hill.

We got about five yards.

15

DON'T JINX YOURSELF

Our captive, who I loosely planned to drop off somewhere near the police station, woke up. Jermaine had taken a turn carrying him, the lightweight man thrown over one shoulder like a sack of corn.

Unnoticed, he came to and started screaming blue murder. He was heard instantly, the sound of his troops rallying to follow us into the fog enough to make us start running.

"Ooh, me bunion," cried Gloria, huffing along at her best pace.

There was no chance we could outrun them, finding motorised transport on which we could escape was never going to happen, and hiding did not sound like a great option either.

Thankfully, I suppose, we didn't have to decide what to do. We didn't even have to find a way to silence Tommy DeMeco because he stopped yelling at the exact same moment we all stopped running.

In the street before us as it swept downhill and back toward the town centre, a line of pirate figures was emerging from the mist. They were five yards away and still indistinct, but we could see enough detail to know they were not tourists or villagers dressed up to join in the festival activities later today.

No, we were staring at the same awful, nightmarish characters we'd encountered in Edward's house barely twelve hours ago.

Around their necks hung the same frayed nooses, the loose end hanging to the ground in some cases. Each held a cutlass or an old flintlock pistol – some had both, and their deathly eyes were fixed on us with a message that needed no translation.

Peter Webster asked, "Who are these guys?"

Molly swore and Barbie echoed it.

Could it get any worse?

You know how they say to not jinx yourself by asking stupid question like if things can get worse?

Tommy DeMeco had yelled for his men to come get him and just when I was gawping in mute disbelief at the 'ghosts' to our front, his gun-toting hoodlums burst into sight behind us.

We were trapped between ghost pirates and homicidal gangsters.

There were twenty or so of Tommy's men and about a dozen ghosts. I don't know who shot first, but I think it was DeMeco's guys.

Jermaine piled into me, driving the air from my lungs as he herded me to find cover. I heard the whip of a bullet passing through the air close to my head and then we were off the street, running down an alleyway between houses.

Behind us in the street, a cacophony of shooting and shouting erupted.

The firefight didn't last long, the shooting from Tommy's men dying away as they ran back into the mist, presumably heading for the nightclub and the cover it provided.

We reached the end of the alley to discover it was a dead end. It led to the gardens behind the houses at this end of Torruga. We needed to find a way to get back to the town centre, but hidden in the mist were people dressed as ghostly pirates and I knew they meant us harm.

I didn't believe for one moment that they had arrived outside Strawberry Moons nightclub by accident. They knew we were there and had come to deal with us. Inadvertently we had lifted the lid on something that other people wanted to keep hidden and now we were in real trouble.

My phone rang, the trill sound too loud in the quiet we were trying to maintain. I snatched it from my pocket, saw Alistair's name displayed, and rejected the call. I knew why he was calling me – he'd heard gunfire and assumed I was at the centre of it. I could have felt insulted were his assumption not one hundred percent accurate.

To top off the phone giving away our position, Tommy managed to wriggle free of Jermaine's grip too. In a moment of confusion where Hideki and Barbie came to help Jermaine and all three ended up getting in each other's way, the pint-sized gang boss slipped free and started running.

Despite a limp, inflicted when Hideki dropped him from the first-floor fire escape no doubt, Tommy got away. He was heading back toward the street where we last saw the 'ghosts' and it would have been folly to follow him.

His voice carried back through the mist.

"I'm going to find Edward Teach before you. No one double crosses Tommy DeMeco. No one!"

I had so many questions for him, but it was too late now to hope for any answers. Barbie tugged at my sleeve.

"Come on, Patty! We've gotta go!"

She vaulted a garden fence effortlessly, which I then clambered over. Jermaine lifted Gloria, depositing her on the other side, before leaping over himself. Two gardens over, we found another alleyway. It led back to the street that would take us into town, but was it safe?

There was no sound coming from the street, but we agreed to wait, giving ourselves a minute to get our breath back and to be sure the danger had passed.

My phone continued to buzz in my pocket as Alistair made call after call and others in the group announced the same was happening to them. Our other team would be heading in our direction …

I gasped when I realised that could mean they would run into the ghosts as they returned to town. Jolted by the horrifying thought of Alistair and my friends facing the potentially deadly force, I ran down the rest of the alley and burst into the street.

There was no sign of the ghosts.

Admittedly, I could only see a few yards in any direction just as before, but there was no sound from them either. Wait though. Do ghosts make any noise?

Barbie, Molly, and the others all caught up to me, bursting from the alley just a second or so after me.

"Patty, what is it?" gasped Barbie. "I thought we were going to wait?"

Raising my phone to my ear, I gabbled, "It's Alistair. He must have heard the shots and be heading this way. He could run straight into the ghosts …"

Molly made a small squeak of fright. "I don't think we need to worry about that."

I twisted at the waist, my heart racing again because I knew what I was about to see.

Sure enough, emerging from the mist were the dead and decaying pirates. Closer now, I could see the flesh hanging from their bones and the shrunken nature of the bodies. Too terrified to scream, I watched as they formed a ring around us.

Just like in the corridor outside Tommy DeMeco's office, we found ourselves backing into a circle. The pirates still had their cutlasses and pistols; weapons that were easily enough to end our lives even with the likes of Jermaine and Hideki among us.

I turned my head, intending to apologise to Barbie and everyone else. I had led them back into the street. If I had just waited like we planned maybe we would have been safe, but before I could speak two things happened.

The first was the realisation that we were missing someone. Peter Webster, a little overweight and very much out of shape, had been huffing and panting along with the rest of us when we escaped the nightclub. He was still with us when we ran down the alleyway and started hopping over garden fences.

He wasn't with us now though. Idly I hoped he might have been able to escape, but the thought left my head as quickly as it had formed when the second thing happened.

16

MOOSE TESTICLES

A sound like a … how the heck could I possibly describe it? From deep in the mist, a hundred yards away, but coming closer at a speed that defied logic was a noise that had to be made by a man, but nevertheless sounded like a moose might if someone set fire to its testicles.

Everyone heard it, so it wasn't like I had imagined it.

I could not help but watch in rapt fascination as the ghosts all froze. They looked at one another, each silently asking if anyone knew what was happening. They had no more idea than us.

The bellowing, bugling noise roared ever closer, and just before it burst from the mist, the tinging sound of the bell from a child's bicycle rang just once.

When it finally exploded into sight, I understood how it had been going so fast, but the incredulity I felt trebled instantly.

Careening toward us were two rickshaws, the men sitting astride the bikes pedalling hell for leather and aiming directly for the ghosts.

Barbie punched the air with both fists and whooped.

Molly yelled, "Who are those guys?"

Jermaine said, "Well I never."

I knew who they were, I just couldn't believe my eyes.

The nearest of the ghosts got enough time to think about the fact that they were about to get mangled before the rickshaw riders ploughed straight into them. I heard a sickening crunch as a haymaker punch swung through the air to connect with a ghostly head and any doubt I may have ever harboured about the supernatural nature of our attackers vanished when I heard the 'ghost' cry out in pain.

Having carved a gap through the ring of dead pirates, the rickshaw riders hit the brakes, skidding to a stop while simultaneously leaning hard to one side to slew the back end of their carriages around.

The rider nearest me bellowed, "Get on!" even though everyone was already moving. Everyone but me it seemed. My feet were rooted to the ground, the signal from my brain to make them move getting lost somewhere on its way.

Taking my terrified breaths in relieved gulps, I locked eyes with Tempest Michaels when he took a fleeting second to look my way and wink. Then hands bundled me onto the rickshaw as we all scrambled to fit six people onto rickshaws designed for two.

Already facing back down the hill, the 'ghosts' had overcome their stunned surprise and were moving to cut off our escape.

Peddling the other rickshaw, Tempest's right hand man, Big Ben, had to duck when a sword scythed toward his head. Lancing out an arm, he caught the hand that held the sword, grasping it around the wrist and holding on so the 'ghost' was yanked from his feet.

It made the rickshaw hard to steer but none of the other 'ghosts' could get to Big Ben on that side now.

In the bedlam of his struggle, the 'ghost' lost his mask and in panic tried to hide his face. I saw it though and with a jolt that felt like electricity surging directly into my heart, I recognised who it was. Not only that, up close I could see through the costume he wore. The bones and decaying flesh weren't real.

I mean, I'd known that all along, obviously, but it was nice to have my beliefs reaffirmed.

In the next instant, the trailing edge of the noose the 'ghost' wore around his neck caught under the rickshaw's back wheel and he was wrenched from Big Ben's grip.

Big Ben uttered something colourful, disappointed about losing a subject he planned to interrogate, but with the rickshaw now rattling down the hill at speed, we were clear of the danger, and I finally felt safe.

That was when the full impact of the last half an hour hit me, and I threw up over the side of the carriage.

"Ewww," squealed Barbie - I was crammed in next to her with Hideki hanging onto the other side.

Ahead of us, Tempest Michaels was beginning to slow, checking over his shoulder to make sure we had stuck right on his tail. Big Ben's rickshaw with us on board was a few yards back, just close enough for us to be able to see them.

The 'ghosts' had been left well behind and that was making everyone else feel safe. Not me though. When Tempest waved his arm to tell Big Ben to slow down and began to do so himself, I yelled for them to keep going.

"No! Don't slow down! Keep going to the port. We'll meet Alistair and the others there!" My hands were scrambling to get my phone, but Barbie was arguing.

"Patty, we left them a mile behind us. They can't catch us now. It's not safe to go this fast in the fog."

"They can catch us," I assured her. "They have quad bikes."

She frowned at me. "How, Patty? Only the police ..." her voice trailed off as she got what I was telling her.

I nodded my head. My shaking fingers, barely controllable as the adrenaline seeped away to leave me feeling utterly spent, had just hit the button to connect to my boyfriend, but I had time to answer her unspoken question.

"The one whose mask came off. That was the cop who came to get me from my cell last night and again this morning. There is no chance I am wrong. Edward said he thought there might be some dirty cops. I guess he was right."

The rickshaws barrelled on, the two men from the Blue Moon

Detective Agency guiding them through the fog with apparent ease. They would have a story to tell when we stopped. For now though, with Alistair's voice coming through my phone, I needed to explain events to him.

17

SILVESTRE

More than a mile from the events unravelling in the town of Torruga and oblivious to everything beyond his current task, Xavier Silvestre slipped out from his hiding place. More than an hour he'd been waiting for the nurse to decide he needed to use the facilities.

Silvestre's legs were cramping, but he wasted no time trying to massage life back into his sore muscles. There was too little time to spare for such indulgences.

He couldn't be sure that the uncut gems taken from Finn Murphy's body were down here in the sickbay somewhere, but it made sense for them to be kept with the rest of the man's personal effects. From carefully quizzing Dr Nakamura a few hours ago, he knew Finn Murphy's clothing and everything else that had been found on him was locked in a security box in the morgue.

What the good doctor had failed to explain, and then hastily changed the subject about was how they came to identify the body. Silvestre hadn't pursued it because he knew it would tip his hand to do so. However, when the doctor revealed that the body had been found without any form identification on it, he chose to pose one simple question.

"How did you figure out who it was then?"

Dr Nakamura, caught out by his own lie, had floundered. Flustered, if only for a moment, he'd concocted another lie – that Patricia Fisher had been able to figure it out.

There was more to the story than Silvestre had first realised, but until he got Patricia Fisher alone and was able to prise from her everything she wanted to keep secret, he would not know if it was just that they had found his wallet or passport and they were lying about it, or if indeed they had found much, much more.

With the nurse out of the way and a maximum window of about two minutes, Silvestre hurtled through the sickbay door. He'd been watching from a vantage point down the corridor, his Professor Noriega disguise still in place, and knew there was no one else inside.

Except, when he got into the reception area of the ship's main medical facility, he realised he was wrong. One of the beds was occupied.

Skidding to a stop, Silvestre held his breath and watched. The old man appeared to be asleep, his chest rising and falling rhythmically to the accompanying sound of a quiet snore.

The treasure hunter took his hand from the hilt of the knife on his belt and hustled through the door to the morgue at the back of the room.

The earlier visit had been a scouting mission as much as anything else. He wanted to see Finn Murphy's body because he wanted to be able to remember the man's face. The albino Irishman, whether he knew it at the time or not, was possibly the man who discovered the whereabouts of the treasure taken from the hold of the San José, one of the most famous lost treasure vessels to have ever sailed.

Xavier Silvestre knew that if he was able to pick up Murphy's trail and trace it back to where he had been, history would record his name, not Murphy's as the one who found the treasure. He would be famous, a household name in his home nation, and toasted around the world. He was already rich, but the treasure, even after he'd been forced to share it under the rules of maritime recovery, would make him one of the richest men in Spain, if not Europe.

Fame and money. What more could a man ask for?

Thinking the security on the ship laughable – he'd been able to feign leaving his ID in his crew cabin to gain access to the lower decks. To increase his chances, he'd waited until there was a sole crewmember queuing for the elevator who was both young and distracted by their phone. The young man had barely even looked at Silvestre. Dressed as he was in a serious suit and sporting a fake badge created in his cabin to mimic the crew nameplates, his claim to be a doctor and in a hurry was all he needed.

Like peeling back layers, he'd wormed his way through the lax security and now, faced with the security lockers in the morgue, he found the one he wanted was helpfully labelled to show whose belongings were inside it.

Silvestre paused, stilling his breathing to check the nurse was not yet returning - he would hear the toilet flush as a ten second warning. Content he had time, he produced a set of lockpicks and had the security locker open a moment later.

Silently chuckling to himself about how easy they were making it for him, he was cursing in the next breath because the gemstones were not there at all. A swift root around with his hand confirmed the locker contained nothing but the clothing cut from the deceased's body.

Grimacing, he racked his brain, questioning where else they might be, but the sound of the toilet flushing farther down the corridor outside jolted him back into action.

He closed the locker, backtracked through the morgue doors and was about to cross the sickbay itself when the phone at the medic's desk rang.

The unexpected sound in the quiet room startled the old man, waking him from his slumber. Now sitting up in bed, Silvestre placed his hand back on the hilt of his knife. However, his half-planned idea to silently kill the patient and escape was dashed when he heard the nurse running to get to the phone before it cut off.

Silently cursing, Xavier Silvestre backed away from the morgue doors and looked for somewhere to wait.

18

BUILT-IN COMPASS

As you might imagine, the moment we stopped, I wanted to know how it was that two men from the Blue Moon Paranormal Detective Agency came to be rescuing us thousands of miles from their office in England.

Barbie pulled a sheepish face and put her hand up. "I sent them a message," she admitted.

I had to ask, "When?"

"Last night. Right when everything was getting super creepy, and the police turned up but then arrested us. I sent Big Ben a text saying we had just encountered a bunch of deadly ghost pirates in a tropical paradise and asked if they were busy."

Tempest frowned at his partner. "That's not what you told me."

Hideki asked, "Why do you have his number?"

Big Ben smiled like a wolf that had cornered a lamb, and it was aimed directly at Barbie.

"You appear to be missing your bra."

Barbie blushed and I noticed Hideki frowning.

Tempest clicked his fingers, his own frown deepening. "Hey, earth to Ben."

Big Ben finally blinked and looked away from my blonde friend. "Hmmm?"

Tempest growled, "You said Patricia and her friends were in dire straits and needed our help. That's quite far removed from 'are we busy?' don't you think?"

Big Ben shrugged. "Barbie made it sound important. I was left with the impression she would owe me a favour if I came to her aid." Big Ben double pumped his eyebrows at Barbie meaningfully and Hideki swung his gaze to check how she was reacting.

She looked a little breathless, that being the effect Big Ben has on most women.

"How did you even get here so fast?" I wanted to know. "There's no airport."

Tempest cocked an eyebrow. "Seaplane?"

"Oh. Yes, I suppose that would work."

Tempest continued, "We hopped on a commercial jet to Portugal last night – it's only a couple of hours from Gatwick - and convinced a chap with a seaplane to run us out here. We arrived an hour ago."

I was fairly sure that had come at quite a price. I'd never been in a seaplane, but had to imagine a private charter to an island in the middle of the Atlantic Ocean was anything but cheap. We would discuss it later. I had other questions first.

"Okay, so you got a message and flew straight here without hesitating. I thank you for that, but how did you find us so quickly?"

Big Ben patted his groin and aimed it at Barbie, claiming, "I followed my built-in compass. It always points directly at the biggest pair of ti …"

"Will you pack it in?" grumbled Tempest, cutting Big Ben off before he could complete what he was saying. Frowning at his partner, but turning his attention to me, he said, "We stood on the dock and listened. When the shooting started, we 'borrowed' a couple of rickshaws and hauled butt."

Big Ben clapped his hands together. "One rescue in the bag. Tequilas all round, yes? I believe I can see a bar from here, actually." He twisted his feet to face the direction he wanted to go and crooked his arm to invite Barbie to take his elbow. "Come along, Blondie. We can discuss my reward."

Hideki stepped into his path.

"I'm her boyfriend," he stated. It did not come across as a threat. More like a gentle warning to behave.

Big Ben smiled. "We'll see."

Before that situation could escalate, the sound of feet moving at a jogging pace reached our ears just before Alistair and the other team parted the mist. They were coming from the town back to the docks.

They already knew the shooting they heard was aimed at us – sort of, but also knew we were all unharmed. Quite how we escaped without a scratch required some explanation.

Alistair pulled me into a hug. "Are you truly all okay?" he asked, his voice a murmur next to my ear as he held me tight against his body. "I rather like the pirate wench outfit, by the way. You can wear that later when this is all over if you like."

I felt my cheeks warming and turned away from him to face the rest of the team. Alistair acted like nothing had happened and spoke to the group at a normal volume.

"You said on the phone you got caught between some ghosts and some gangsters, did I hear that right?"

Our phone call had been brief; just long enough for me to cover the salient points. Now he wanted some detail.

Pushing back to get some distance between us, I said, "Yes. That's right. You're going to ask how we got away, and the answer is we got rescued."

Alistair had never met Tempest Michaels or his oversized companion, Big Ben, and I could not recall if I had ever mentioned them to him. I met Tempest when I rented the office he used to occupy. It was firebombed in an incident a year before I came across it – some evil clowns with a revenge issue were behind the damage.

He has dachshunds too, which made for a coincidence that got us talking. That might have been the end of our interaction, but a few weeks later I arrived at the scene of a murder to find the paranormal investigator already there. We were both working the same case, but for different clients.

I'd worked with him a couple of times and our paths had crossed more times than I cared to count. That he was here in the British Union Isles was something I was still struggling to wrap my head around, and now I had to explain it to Alistair.

Tempest stepped forward, his hand extended. "Tempest Michaels."

"Alistair Huntley," replied my boyfriend. "I believe I owe you a debt of gratitude."

Tempest dipped his head in acknowledgement, but said, "It was the least I could do for an old friend."

His comment drew a raised eyebrow from Alistair and prompted a hurried explanation about how we had met.

Big Ben, I noticed, shook Alistair's hand when his name came up, but was generally too busy checking out Molly and Deepa. Like Tempest, he was dressed for action, both men wearing hardwearing, black combat trousers and boots beneath skin-tight, dark grey t-shirts. They had packs on their backs, also black, which seemed to form the entirety of their luggage, and they were constantly vigilant. The trait of observing and assessing everyone and everything around them was something I had spotted back when I first met them. They were ex-military and quite serious people. Barbie and Molly had made sure to regale Alistair's team with a complete run down of our morning's activities, including the horror of Tommy DeMeco and his gang, and the 'ghosts' we ran into.

At the mention of ghosts, Tempest grinned to himself.

"If you are going to tell me they were not ghosts, you can save your breath," I told him. Turning to Alistair, I revealed, "They were the police."

The captain of the Aurelia twitched, his jaw dropping open. "The police?"

I shrugged. "One of them was for sure. His mask came off. It was the same officer who collected me from my cell last night and he knows I recognised him."

Alistair huffed out a breath. "This is bad." It was a classic understatement. Now gathered all in one group, Alistair looked around at both teams and the Blue Moon chaps. "Ensign Sam Chalk is still out there somewhere, but we are up against superior forces and if the police are against us, we are on shaky ground. Most of you are my crew, and the order I am giving now is to return to the ship. I want all members of the Aurelia's crew to depart the island now. Mrs Fisher and I will remain here and attempt to ascertain where Sam Chalk is. If he is being held by someone, we will arrange for his release …"

Guardedly, because he was talking to his captain, Lieutenant Commander Martin Baker asked, "What if we choose to stay, Sir?"

Alistair stopped what he was saying, slowly rotating his head to look at the other members of his crew.

"Does anyone else wish to disobey a direct order?"

"Yes, Sir," replied Deepa without needing to think, Martin's wife reaching out to thread her hand into her husband's.

"Me too," agreed Barbie just before everyone else echoed the sentiment.

Alistair nodded his head, accepting the news with a wry smile before turning back to answer Martin's question.

"You asked what if you choose to stay? Then you prove yourself worthy of the rank you wear. All of you do and you have my heartfelt thanks."

Molly raised her hand. "What do we do now though?" Her question was aimed at me more than anyone else. "I thought we ran out of clues to follow already? It was supposed to be that DeMeco fella who had Sam, but he wasn't there."

"That's right," I replied, all eyes in the group looking my way. "We hit a dead end with that lead, and I fear we may have stirred up a hornet's nest. I doubt Mr DeMeco will choose to spend the rest of today watching daytime TV."

"You think he might come after us?" questioned Molly.

Martin answered for me, "It's what bad guys do."

Turning to Alistair, I asked, "How did your lead pan out?"

He huffed out a breath, his expression answering my question before he spoke. "It was nothing. Just a lot of rumour and conjecture. A total waste of our time."

"We ought not to hang around in plain sight," I remarked. "Even if DeMeco doesn't have his men out looking for us, and even if it's not Chief Quimby behind the ghosts who just attacked us, this is still a hostile environment. Someone wants to stop us from finding Edward Teach and whatever it was he was into that got him kidnapped."

"Wait, where's Peter?" squeaked Barbie, finally noticing that the man we rescued from Tommy DeMeco was no longer with us.

Alistair wasn't the only one who felt it necessary to ask, "Who's Peter?"

19

UNHINGED

In the cabin he shared with Angelica Howard-Box, Jordan was once again questioning why he hadn't already run away from the increasingly unhinged woman. Angelica Howard-Box was hellbent on revenge and while Jordan had been a willing part in her schemes so far, he could not help but feel that the net was closing in on her.

If she was caught and he was still with her, he would be unable to deny whatever charges they brought against him. He cursed his luck that he hadn't taken the opportunity to depart already. He could have snuck away when they were in Lanzarote - no one on the crew was looking for him. They were looking for Angelica.

However, his passport had mysteriously gone missing, and he was absolutely certain Angelica had it. She played the innocent when he asked her if she knew where it was, and because she never left the cabin, he had not been able to search her things for it.

Effectively trapped by his deranged employer, even if he left the ship, which he couldn't because one needed a passport to get through the security check, he could not then board a plane to return to England. However, that was something of a moot problem at the moment because they were docked at a tiny island too small to be serviced by aircraft that could fly him home.

Accepting his fate, Jordan was playing along.

Angelica emerged from the bedroom. She was wearing that sapphire necklace still, the one she took from Patricia Fisher and had been wearing ever since. Jordan had no idea what the significance of the item might be, but he noted that she was also wearing Patricia Fisher's clothes again. That he had helped Angelica break into the Windsor Suite, overpower the Butler who opened the door, and then destroyed or stole almost everything the woman owned was another thing playing on his conscience.

He'd been a criminal for as long as he could remember, but what he was doing now appeared to have no financial gain attached to it. He was being paid by the psycho woman he now shared a cabin with - she had moved in with him when they caught wind the crew was searching for her by going cabin to cabin, but it wasn't enough to convince him to stick around any longer than he absolutely had to.

Angelica was motivated purely by revenge, her hatred for Patricia Fisher so all-encompassing that no other thoughts entered her head. Jordan questioned if the woman would even remember to eat if he did not semi regularly return to the cabin with food.

"Did you call him?" Angelica asked.

Jordan nodded and said, "Yes."

"Why is he not here then?" Angelica wanted to know, irritation evident in the tone of her voice.

A flippant remark formed on Jordan's lips, and he had to bite down to keep it inside. Angelica always expected everything to happen exactly as she wanted it to happen, and within seconds of her making a request.

"He said he would be here as soon as he could, but that he was engaged in his duties as a member of the security team."

"Everyone has an excuse," Angelica remarked in a bored manner.

Jordan shook his head. "If he abandons his post, it will be

noticed. He's supposed to be keeping a low profile, isn't he? Those were your instructions," Jordan pointed out.

He knew he had scored a point, but he also understood it had been a foolish thing to do.

Angelica's head snapped around, her accusing eyes pinning Jordan in place with the intensely fiery rage burning within them.

"Don't you get it!" she raged. "She's winning. That blonde bimbo is still by her side. You were supposed to break them up. It was a simple enough task," Angelica sneered down her nose. "All you had to do was create a false email, but even that proved too complicated for you, didn't it?"

She was being ridiculously unfair. Jordan knew that with absolute certainty just as he knew that defending himself was pointless. Angelica never listened to anything that anyone else said. Nevertheless, he could not help himself when he pointed out how wrong she was.

"You dictated the email to me, Angelica. I did precisely as you asked me to. That it did not work is not my fault."

"Then you did it wrong. You claim to know how to hack a computer, yet Patricia Fisher is still employed as the ship's detective and her friends are still at her side. Worse yet, she is still involved with the captain." Angelica stalked across the small cabin as she talked, her movements jerky and spasmodic as her fingers clenched in the air with her frustration. "It is time for me to strike a heftier blow."

Jordan did not like the sound of that. He was a computer hacker and a thief. He did not go in for violence and never had. It was only when Angelica wafted a significant amount of money under his nose that he agreed to go along with the raid on her suite. He had wielded the stun gun, holding a weapon for the first time in his life. He had never felt so nervous, and though it had worked perfectly, robbing the tall Jamaican butler of consciousness before he could even react, Jordan had no intention of ever repeating such an act regardless of how much money Angelica offered him.

Unable to stop himself, he asked, "What are you going to do?"

The rage dominating Angelica's face dropped away, the grimace tightening her eyes softened to be replaced by a smile.

"Taking her friends away didn't work. Taking her lover away didn't work. And taking her career away didn't work. However, I have left the best until last. There is something else that she loves, loves in a way that transcends human interaction. She has no children who I could target, but that does not mean that she is without dependants."

Jordan knew what Angelica was proposing without her needing to spell it out. She had talked about it before. Hearing her announce it now sealed the decision in his head - he had to get away from her. He didn't know how he was going to do it, but even if he couldn't find his passport, he was going to hack into the ship's system, erase any trace that he had ever been on board, and vanish.

He had the beginnings of a plan lurking in the back of his head. He'd been thinking about it for some time, and only fear of his employer had kept him from investigating whether it was possible or not. Now faced with the very real possibility that she was going to get him caught or killed, Jordan knew it was time to go for broke.

A knock at the door disturbed his thoughts and the familiar voice of Angelica's tame security officer echoed in the passageway outside.

20

EDWARD'S HOUSE

I explained about Peter on our way back to Edward's house. None of us had seen him sneak away, but we all agreed that he had been with us right up until we found ourselves surrounded by the 'ghosts'.

What he had been doing in the company of Tommy DeMeco and why he was being tortured for information remained a mystery. Much like the entire case regarding Edward, I had no interest in trying to solve it. My sole focus was still on locating Sam and getting him back.

Discovering that at least some members of the local Police Department were involved in whatever was going on vindicated my decision to go at this myself.

"But you think Peter escaped?" Tempest sought to confirm what I believed.

I gave him a sort of half shrug. "I don't think Tommy DeMeco's men would have been able to regain him. When we last saw him, they had retreated back towards the nightclub. I don't think the ghosts got him either, though I cannot be sure what happened after we fled the area."

Tempest remarked, "It's all very strange. What was it you said Peter Webster did again?"

"He said he was an accountant." I recalled what Peter said and how he said it and the back of my skull itched. Why was that? What was it about Peter that meant something? Did it have anything to do with Sam going missing?

I concentrated on the problem, but no answer would come.

Leaving the docks, Tempest and Big Ben led us to where they 'borrowed' the rickshaws. The owners started out looking angry, but an apology both in verbal and cash form swiftly placated them. More so when additional cash appeared because we needed to hire more rickshaws to transport us back up the winding path to Edward's house.

It was quiet in the mist which was showing no sign of dissipating even though it was nearing midday. The cover it provided remained a blessing. Sitting next to Alistair, we enjoyed a few minutes respite from the drama of our day. Slipping my hand into his, we could have been on a romantic getaway were it not for the fact that Sam was still missing, and we were very much hip deep in someone else's escapade.

We stayed like that until the gate of Edward's cliffside mansion appeared through the mist. Of course, at no point during the ride was my mind at rest; I was spending every waking moment attempting to unpick the strange case in which we had unintentionally become embroiled.

Though I wasn't consciously trying to solve it, more and more I was questioning whether I would have to. Where was Sam? Who had him? Edward was mixed up in something, there could be no doubt about that. Members of the local constabulary plus a local criminal gang wanted to know where he was.

Edward and Sam had been missing for almost eighteen hours now, long enough for all sorts of terrible things to have happened to them. I pushed that awful thought from my head and squinted into the mist.

What secrets would we find inside Edward's house?

Tempest appeared by my left ear, causing me to squeal in fright when he spoke.

"We are going to drop short here at the gate," he announced.

I raised my eyebrows. "Drop short?" What did that mean?

Quickly, Tempest explained. "This is where the attack took place last night, yes?" He already knew the answer to that and didn't bother to wait for me to reply. "If it is known that you are poking around, which it clearly is, this would be an obvious place for them to post someone on lookout. Big Ben and I will skirmish forward to give the grounds a quick once over. If there's someone here waiting to report your arrival, I'd like to know about it before they have the chance."

Tempest had been in the lead rickshaw with Big Ben, his tall colleague appearing out of the mist with Martin and Deepa. When they stopped, everyone else had been forced to halt behind them. Now everyone was getting out of their rickshaws and questioning what was going on.

When Tempest explained, Martin immediately volunteered to go with him. It prompted everyone including Gloria to volunteer too.

Tempest smiled and scratched his head when the octogenarian put her hand up to perform a reconnaissance patrol of Edward's grounds then politely turned her down.

"More than a couple of us and we risk being spotted. I'll go with Martin," he slapped the leader of my security team on his left shoulder and started moving, giving no opportunity for anyone to raise an argument or counterproposal.

The rickshaw drivers were handed a wad of cash each and sent on their way. I watched the mist swallow them once more as the bikes wobbled back down the dirt track towards the town.

I had no idea how long it might take for Tempest and Martin to comb the grounds, vast and ornamental as they were, and was thankful when they returned just a shade more than five minutes later.

"There doesn't appear to be anyone waiting for us," reported

Tempest. "I cannot, however, rule out that someone is hiding in the house, it's quite clear that it has been visited in the last few hours."

He was already starting to walk backwards up the path towards Edward's house, the thick mist beginning to envelope him. Like everyone else, I hurried to follow, asking for clarification as we went.

"Someone has been here? How can you tell?"

It was Martin who answered, "The front door to the house is wide open and there are several sets of footsteps leaving paths across the grass. It looks like someone was searching the grounds for something. And they were almost certainly in the house before that."

We were not cautious in approaching the house. Tempest was leading the way, his confident strides crunching the gravel under foot as he led our group directly toward the front door. Just as Martin had said, it was wide open though Jermaine closed it once we were all inside.

Ahead of us was the kitchen where we had gathered for Edward to pass out drinks and where he had begun to tell us about what he wanted me to investigate. There were doors to our left and right, most of which were closed, but Tempest wasn't wrong about there having been visitors.

The house had been tossed.

Drawers were open even on the console table to the right of us in the lobby. There were things on the floor where someone had indiscriminately rooted through it. I suspected we would find much worse farther into the house.

Big Ben called to Tempest, "Sentry?"

Tempest, already moving away from the front door, replied, "Yes, please."

I wasn't sure what that meant, but as we filtered into the house, Big Ben tapped Schneider on the shoulder.

"Hey, big fella." Lieutenant Schneider was almost as tall and as broad as the Blue Moon detective. "There's too much territory to cover. I could do with a couple of volunteers to help me watch over the grounds."

Schneider dipped his head. "Of course. Pippin. Molly." Both

spun around at the sound of their names. "Let's make sure no one can sneak up on us."

The four of them went to the stairs, ascending them as the rest of us left the lobby behind. I was heading back toward the point where we found Sam's magnifying glass.

Barbie was with me. "What do you need me to do, Patty? You want me to find his computer?"

Tempest, who was a few yards away, twisted around to respond.

"Oh, yes. You're a whizz with a computer. I forgot about that. I was going to do it myself, but I'm not the best. Back in England …"

"You have Jane do it," Barbie finished his sentence.

He and I had only worked together briefly, but the strengths of each team had been displayed and learned quickly.

"There has to be an office here somewhere," Tempest looked around.

We were still in the central hallway that ran through the house and what we wanted could be behind any of the doors. It could be upstairs or downstairs, and the sense of urgency brought about by Tempest's suggestion that the house might be under observation did nothing to quell my desire to find it quickly.

"Everyone, split up," I begged. "Look for an office. We didn't see one last night, but if there is evidence to be found regarding whatever Edward is caught up in, that's where I expect to find it."

With so many of us splitting off to explore the house, it wasn't long before someone opened the right door. As luck would have it, it was Barbie who chanced upon the right room. Tucked away at the back of the house where it overlooked the garden, the office was a hub of destruction.

As if a small tornado had chosen to touch down inside Edward's office, the contents were strewn everywhere.

Stopped in the doorway while Barbie began to make her way through the mess, I called out loudly so that everyone would know, "We've found it!"

Jermaine and Alistair were the first to arrive, catching up to me in the doorway just as I was beginning to pick a path through the destruction inside.

It wasn't a large room when compared to the rest of the house, but was nevertheless larger than the size of an average person's living room. In the centre, a large mahogany desk dominated the space. It was set so a person sitting at the desk would have their back to the door. Along both sides of the room were ceiling height book-cases, the contents of which were largely spilled onto the carpet.

In the left hand pedestal of the desk cabinet Barbie found a filing cabinet. The lock on it had been forced, the tooth marks left behind by a small crowbar evident in the delicate wood.

That someone had been here looking for something did not need to be stated.

Deepa and Gloria arrived, the latter holding a bottle of whisky in her right hand and a glass in the left. Tempest appeared in the doorway just a moment later. By then, Barbie had righted the upturned office chair and was coaxing the computer into life.

"At least it still works," she remarked when the screen bloomed into life.

Tempest came to stand by my shoulder, joining me in looking around the mess that was once an organised office.

"The question is," he murmured, "did they find what they were looking for? And if they did, did they take it with them?"

We all knew that the only way we were going to find that out was by doing what we could to sift through the papers thrown all over the floor. Without feeling the need for conversation, we all got on our hands and knees and began to search.

21

A SECRET WORTH KEEPING

We were as hasty as we could be, but time ticked away and even with so many of us looking, we were finding nothing.

Barbie reported, “There’s nothing on this computer.”

“It’s been wiped?” asked Tempest.

She spun around in the chair to face him. “No, I mean there’s just nothing of worth on it. It’s been used but only for a few emails – none of them recently. There are some files too, but I could only find two that have been opened in the last month and both were outlines for a book he is planning to write.”

“I found this, madam,” announced Jermaine, holding up pieces of paper held together by a staple. “It appears to be a denied loan application. The amount is two million pounds.”

My eyebrows were not the only ones that shot skyward. Barbie bounced out of her chair to look over Jermaine’s find.

“This is recent,” she read from the paper. “Less than three months ago.” She went back to her chair, clicking the mouse to bring up a file. “Why would they deny him a loan? He’s seriously rich. I mean … just look at this place,” she indicated the house. “Surely, he could use it as collateral?”

Alistair asked a different question. "Why would he even need a loan?"

No one had an answer and we searched for a few more minutes to be sure there was nothing of worth in the room. I say *we* searched, but *I* wasn't doing that at all. I was thinking.

I sat back on my haunches and sucked on my teeth.

"We're looking in the wrong place," I tested my conclusion and decided it held water. "There's another office somewhere."

Deepa argued, "We already searched the house."

I grabbed a bookshelf to lever myself upright, grunting at the effort it took and gladly accepting Alistair's hand when he beat Jermaine in coming to my aid.

"It's not in the house," I announced, employing my need to be cryptic.

Questions followed me, Barbie calling out to ask where I was going and what I was talking about as I left Edward's office without another word.

That someone had been in the house searching for something they expected to find in his office was obvious. Who they were remained a mystery, but I was willing to bet they hadn't found what they wanted.

I needed to see if my hunch was right, but I remembered something else on my way and waited for the others to catch up.

"We'll need a pry bar or a hammer perhaps," I remarked.

"Patty, what are you up to?" Barbie wanted to know.

Alistair agreed with her thoughts on the matter. "Yes, dear, you are being unusually cryptic."

"I might be wrong," I admitted. "I spotted a door with a padlock on it last night. There were no cobwebs around the door and the padlock looked new. I think the police or DeMeco's gang or heck maybe even someone else we don't yet know about was in here looking for something."

Tempest produced a multitool from his backpack and Jermaine found a hefty looking meat tenderiser in a kitchen drawer. Tooled up, I led the party outside to the outbuilding with the generator. It was still running, making it hard to hear each other.

I was shouting when I pointed to the door. "If Edward has secrets worth keeping, they might be in there."

Tempest held up his multi-tool, eyeing it sceptically – it wasn't up to the task. Neither was the meat tenderiser, but Deepa found a fire extinguisher in the corner.

"Step aside, boys," she gave them two seconds' warning then swung the heavy object to smash the clasp the padlock went through.

Once the door was opened, we knew we had found what everyone else had been looking for.

"How come they didn't find this last night when they raided the house?" Deepa asked. "They had to come in here to cut the power."

I was heading into the cramped, windowless office, but paused to examine what she had just said. It made the back of my head itch.

"Wow, maps," said Barbie and my focus shifted to see what she was talking about.

Alistair took a fold out map from her as she eased into the office chair in front of a fancy looking computer. It had been opened out on the desk next to the keyboard and had been marked with a felt tip pen.

It was an ordnance survey map of the island.

I raised my eyebrows, encouraging Alistair to speak.

"It says Teach's Reach," he reported, letting go with one hand so he could point to a spot just up the coast from Torruga.

The room was just about big enough for us to all get in so that's what we did. One wall had the same ordnance survey map opened out and stuck to it. It measured about six feet in each direction. On another wall, the one opposite the door, pieces of A4 paper printed from a computer, listed names and addresses.

To the left on the same wall was a small, black and white photograph. It was sellotaped to another piece of A4 on which a handwritten note read 'Samuel Glover'. One thing was clear – Edward had been gathering information and whatever it was about, he wanted to keep it secret.

"I have something here," announced Jermaine. He was leafing

through a stack of printed pages on the desk and had come across an aerial photograph. It was of a piece of coastline.

By holding it up against the ordnance survey map, we were able to figure out which piece of coast it was. A few miles to the north of Torruga, it wasn't so much the coastline that was interesting, but what had been superimposed over the water off the coast.

There could be no doubt what we were looking at – it was an offshore runway.

He held the glossy picture up next to the map in Alistair's hands. Although we did not know what it meant, that the two things were connected was quite apparent. The piece of coastline marked as Teach's Reach was directly adjacent to the runway. In fact, studying the two pictures side by side, it looked like the runway would connect to Teach's Reach.

My skull itched, a sure sign that we were looking at something of huge importance to the case in hand, and a whole stack of clues aligned themselves in my head.

"That's what the money was for!" I blurted when I suddenly made sense of Edward's interaction with a local hoodlum.

All eyes swung my way, including Barbie's who had to swivel her desk chair around to look at me.

"What are you talking about, Patty?" she asked. "What money was for what?"

Hideki understood what I meant. "If someone was proposing to build an offshore runway to service the island, the land where it joined would be worth an absolute fortune. Millions. Goodness, maybe billions." He stuck out an arm to point at the outlined piece of the coast on the map Alistair held. "It's completely undeveloped coast. And it looks quite flat. You could put hotels there. You could put a casino there depending on this island's licencing laws. The opportunities are potentially limitless."

Deepa questioned his thinking. "Surely it's too thin of a strip of land? It can't be more than two or three hundred yards deep before it starts hitting the mountains. And what about connecting it with other towns on the island? Surely the cost of building roads through the island and over those mountains would be prohibitive?"

"Ever been to Miami?" I asked. "How wide is the strip of land where you find Collins Avenue?" I named the spit of land bordering Miami Beach that was filled with enormous hotels stretching into the sky.

My point made and accepted, we all went back to staring at the map.

Alistair murmured a single word, "Money." It was arguably the single biggest driver for crime and murder that there was, swapping places on occasion with love and the consequent betrayal of that love.

The name 'Teach's Reach' was a dead giveaway that Edward was involved at a significant level. This was the sort of opportunity that I could imagine people killing for. But which side of this was Edward on? Someone had ransacked his house looking for information, but were they trying to find out what he was up to, or were they attempting to find a way to leverage their inclusion in his investment opportunity?

Better yet, who were they? Was it the police? Was it Tommy DeMeco and his gang?

I laid out a rough theory. "I believe Edward is behind this. He's the one driving the whole opportunity, using his connections, family name, and influence, to bring investors in so that they will construct the airport. He doesn't have the money to get the airport made himself – who does? But he's savvy enough to have dreamt it up. Or maybe he was approached by someone. Whatever the case, Edward has an opportunity to make a serious amount of money and seal his family's name in history for the next century and beyond. International tourism would open up if long-haul flights could land here. Build a few dozen hotels, landscape the beach, and put in a casino as Hideki suggested, and the island's GDP would soar."

"Does he own the land?" Barbie's question halted everyone's thoughts.

Hideki skewed his lips to one side before saying, "He must do, surely?"

Barbie spun back around to face the computer. "I'm still trying to get into this thing. If I can open his emails, who knows what we might find. Any thoughts on what the password might be?"

I didn't bother to ask if she had searched his desk looking for a slip of paper on which he might have jotted a password – it would have been the first thing she did.

Hideki, Deepa, and Martin all moved to surround her, looking over her shoulders as they discussed what might be important enough to Edward for him to use it as a password.

While they did that, I glanced at Tempest, the one member of our group who hadn't spoken in the last five minutes. Since Alistair picked up the map, the paranormal detective had been squinting at it, but not one word had left his lips.

His expression was one that could only be described as dubious and now that he could feel me looking at him, he chose to express what he was thinking.

"I don't think it's feasible."

It was a broad statement and I had to seek clarification.

"What exactly isn't feasible?"

He stepped forward to poke a finger at the map on the wall.

"The whole thing. There are other offshore runways around the world, right? Dozens of them, in fact, but the size required for the type of jet we are talking about is just too big. The island is basically an extinct volcano, right?"

I nodded. "Okay."

Alistair nodded too. "He's right. The land drops away into the Atlantic too steeply."

"And it's the Atlantic," added Tempest. "Not exactly a mill pond. Even if the land were under the water for them to build on, which I doubt it is …"

Barbie cried out, "Got it!" punching the air in her usual exuberant style. Twisting her head to look over her shoulder, she said, "It was a derivation of Queen Anne's Revenge." When I raised my eyebrows, she supplied, "That was the original Black Beard's ship. You remember that Black Beard's real name is Edward Teach?"

I got it now – the dots lining up.

Her attention was already back on the screen where she was opening files.

"There's one here called 'The Big Scam'," she announced.

Deepa choked on a laugh. "That's fairly damning. The man running the scam is brazen enough to call it what it is."

"Once a pirate, always a pirate," chuckled Gloria. She'd had her boots off to rest her feet and was leaning against the doorframe. I figured she was just taking a load off until I spotted the empty bottle. What had contained dark liquid just a few minutes ago was now empty.

Hoping she had shared it with someone or maybe spilled it, I asked, "Any indication who he suckered into it?" I was expecting to discover the chief of police and DeMeco were among the poor saps Edward had conned into investing their money. I could see how the con would work. Edward buys the land, or he already owns it, then he produces a false investor looking to build an airport right next to the land. The land is virtually worthless, but conning people into believing it might be worth an absolute fortune, he passes himself off as a philanthropist and takes their money.

Later he could reveal the investors chose to back out of the plan. Maybe he already had and that was why DeMeco wanted his money back. I could see it all and knew there had to have been thousands of other cons run by other people woven throughout history. This was just the latest one.

How many people had he ripped off? Why were they so foolish? Surely, if it had been real, Edward wouldn't have wanted to share with anyone, and they would have been able to see that? Looking up at the wall, I spotted the list of names and addresses again.

"Those are his victims," I commented to myself, going around the desk and squeezing between Deepa and Martin to get a closer look. I started reading names off the list. "Barbie, can you look these people up?"

Duncan Spencer, the first name on the list, got an immediate hit and took Barbie to a document inside the 'Big Scam' folder that showed all the other names. They were all islanders and the file listed amounts next to their names. They were all big numbers even though only a few of them were over seven figures.

Reeling from our discovery, I asked, "Can you look up Samuel Glover, please?"

I stared at the black and white photograph, listening to Barbie's fingers dance across the keyboard.

When she said, "Oh," as a sort of gasp, I knew what she was going to say. "He's dead. I have a copy of his obituary. I think … yes, there's a scanned copy of a land registration document. He was the original owner of that land on the map."

We all fell silent for a moment. A silence that was broken when Alistair said, "Edward Teach killed him to get the land."

I jumped on that idea, spinning around to lock eyes with Barbie. "Is there anything to indicate Edward is the new landowner? Another land registration document?"

I held my breath and watched as Barbie navigated around the computer's file system. After a minute or so, she said, "Maybe there will be something in the emails."

She clicked the icon to open his mail, the screen filling with the familiar pattern of inbox and unread correspondence above folders of saved messages and read ones that were yet to be archived or deleted.

I came around the desk as we all crammed in around her. There was nothing that looked to be about land ownership, but in Edward's inbox, one name stuck out instantly. I didn't have to ask Barbie to click on it, she was already doing so.

"This is from two days ago," Barbie read from the screen.

We all leaned in close, forming a huddle around her as we read.

That Chief Quimby was involved was already in little doubt in my head – his desire to know where Edward Teach had gone made him too curious to be ignored. The email was from him, and though it demanded Edward meet him so they could discuss his concerns, there was nothing in the email that could connect him to a crime.

Barbie scrolled down the screen a little, selecting another email from the chief of police. We were going backward through an argument raging between the two. It was curious though. Edward was the aggressor, his language far harder and more forceful. In contrast, Chief Quimby appeared to be attempting to placate Edward. There was more than one invitation to meet.

However, when Barbie displayed what was perhaps the fifth or sixth email between the two, my theory about what we were witness to changed irrevocably.

"Alistair, darling," I murmured. "Do you happen to have a number for the mayor?"

He straightened up, taking his phone from a back pocket. As captain of the ship, he was considered in many of the places we stopped to be something halfway between a diplomat and a celebrity. The captain was regularly wined and dined by local dignitaries who wanted their voters to know the cruise line bringing all the dollars to their shore was being effectively schmoozed.

I was going to tell Angus all that we had found and get his help, but before I could, Tempest's phone rang, an incoming call from Big Ben he told us as he connected the call and put it on speaker.

"Hey, guys!" shouted Big Ben. "We're about to have company!"

22

NOT MY FIRST HAUNTED HOUSE

Martin ran to the door and peered out into the mist. No one breathed.

Over the phone, Big Ben asked, "Fight or run?"

His question drove a spike of fear right through me. I knew the Blue Moon boys were more used to standing their ground. At their core they were still soldiers. Martin and the other security officers were trained for hand-to-hand combat too, and both Jermaine and Hideki … well, you know how well they can fight, but the people coming for us were probably armed.

It could be the police or DeMeco and his men and it didn't really matter which. Heck, if they were both after the same thing, they might even have joined forces.

Tempest took the phone off speaker and put it to his ear instead. I could hear him discussing something with his colleague, the exchange too quiet for me to hear what was being said.

Martin came back inside the brick outhouse. "He's not wrong. There are figures advancing toward the house. It looks like they have fanned out to make sure they surround the whole place."

"Can we get away when they go into the house?" asked Barbie.

Martin looked doubtful. "Maybe, but some of them will pass right by us. If one of them looks inside …"

"We'll be trapped," Barbie finished his sentence.

"And we need to get the others out of the house anyway," I concluded, my heart pounding in my chest.

Gloria, who hadn't spoken in ages and had a happy glow about her from the whisky she'd drunk, was confused about why we were getting worried.

"If we know that Edward stole from them, can't we just explain that we're not involved? They think we've been helping the bad guy. It's no wonder they've been chasing us all day."

I shook my head. "I think it's the other way around, Gloria. I think Edward is the victim."

Barbie snatched a thumb drive from a drawer and stabbed it into one of the computer's USB ports.

"I'm going to save everything I can on to this as a backup," she announced. "And send all of it to the cloud so I can retrieve it later."

Though I had no idea how to do what she had just said and wouldn't be able to retrieve a file from the cloud if my life depended on it – what the heck is the cloud anyway? – I knew why she was doing it. There was too much data on the computer. It would take days to examine each file and we were already out of time.

Tempest ended his call and clicked his fingers twice to make sure we were all listening.

"We're totally surrounded," he announced. "There's no chance we will make it through them." It was a dreadful sentence to hear, yet Tempest looked utterly unshaken by our predicament.

From outside, a voice boomed over a loudspeaker.

"We just want Edward Teach. Tell us where he is, and you can go. We know you helped him to find a hiding place. Is he on your ship? You have two minutes to surrender peacefully. Otherwise, we will storm the house and beat the answers from whoever is left alive."

I strained my hearing, trying to figure out who I was hearing. It sounded like Chief Quimby, but I could not be sure.

Tempest started backing away, heading for the exit and the gardens outside the small building we were in. With his right arm he beckoned we follow.

"Come along, everyone. I rather think we ought to give these chaps the slip."

I wasn't the only confused person.

Barbie said, "I thought you just said we couldn't get through them?"

Ahead of us, Tempest nodded. "That's right. We're going to go under them instead."

Now I was really confused. Especially when he headed for the house. We had to cross twenty yards in the open, the mist helping immensely as we tried to stay out of sight. Inside, Tempest led us to the lobby where at the foot of the stairs he swung around and went up them. We were following, but I had no idea why.

Fortunately, Tempest felt like talking. Gesticulating with his arms as he climbed to the next floor, he said, "The 'ghosts' vanished, right? That's what Martin told me. He was chasing after one and it nicked him with a blade …"

"I'd hardly call it a nick," argued Martin.

Not wanting to get into it, Tempest simply said, "From your description, you were caught off guard. It could have run the sword straight through you but chose to just poke you with it instead. Compared to the injury you could be sporting, I'd call it a nick. Anyway …" Tempest moved the conversation along.

Above us, Molly and Pippin appeared. They had concerned looks on their faces.

Tempest was explaining something, but my brain had gotten itself all caught up with the previous point he made. The 'ghost' could have killed Martin or caused him serious injury, but it didn't. Why? They hadn't looked willing to show us any mercy since.

For that matter, if the 'ghosts' who attacked the house were the police officers involved in Chief Quimby's little plan, why were they looking for Edward? I could only conclude that they didn't have him, but that confused me even more.

The back of my skull itched in a familiar way. I was seeing

something, an important clue that was hiding just out of sight. If I could just concentrate my mind on it …

Molly employed a very rude word, and she was not the only one. My wandering brain had caused my feet to slow so I was at the back of the pack. They were all gasping in shock or surprise at something, but I couldn't see what it was.

"How did you know?" questioned Deepa, her voice filled with wonder.

Tempest chuckled, "This is not my first haunted house."

My friends had gone into a room – it was the one Martin had been in when the 'ghost' disappeared. I knew that much from the snippets of conversation that had drifted unconsciously into my brain while I was pondering the confusing clues. However, my view was blocked by Big Ben and Schneider whose wide backs filled the doorway.

I could still hear Tempest talking. He said, "I'll lead," but it no longer sounded like he was in the room. His voice had taken on an echoey effect, and I was left with the impression that he was farther away from me than the dimensions of the room would allow.

Weaving around and standing on my tiptoes, I could see Jermaine and Alistair, but the press of people in the room appeared to be thinning. I found out why a moment later when Big Ben realised I was trying to see and stepped out of the way.

There was a bed to the right, a large four poster thing with an ornate silk eiderdown covering it. It was the centrepiece of the room, but nothing more than a distraction from the more interesting hole in the wall I could see opposite me.

A bookcase that was clearly supposed to be flush with the wall, had been swung outward to reveal the opening. Jermaine was waiting for me, using his arm to wave Deepa and then Barbie into the secret passageway leading off the room.

I might have been more shocked by its discovery were it not something I had seen before. In the Maharaja's palace in Zangrabar I was attacked by a man who found his way into my room through a secret passage.

"Do we know where it goes?" I asked, the answer coming back from Tempest at the head of the group.

"Not yet."

Jermaine tucked in behind me and Big Ben pulled the bookcase back into place – there was a handle mounted on the back so he could do so. The natural light filtering in from outside was cut off, plunging the passageway into darkness, but plenty of my friends already had their phones out and their torches enabled.

We were inside the walls and out of sight of the people outside. This was good, but my head was still filled with questions.

"How did you know to look for a secret passage," I asked.

I got shushed, someone at the front wanting me to keep quiet. I fell silent, but could tell there was something happening ahead of me and squinted into the semi-darkness until I realised it was the people in front of me squeezing to get around Tempest. He had stopped in the narrow passageway, waiting for me to catch up to him.

Whispering, he said, "Our voices will echo and give away our location if the people outside are in the house." I nodded my understanding. "I figured there had to be a passageway in this room from the way Martin described it. He said the 'ghost' tagged him with the cutlass. Martin obviously thought the 'ghost' was trying to kill him, but I think it was just a distraction so it could escape. All I had to do was light a flame and see which way it guttered. The movement of air through the room pulled me to the bookcase. Like I said, this is not my first haunted house."

Ahead of me, the heads of my friends were disappearing. Vanishing from sight which gave me a start when I first noticed it. They were, of course, not vanishing, but descending a flight of stone stairs. They led down and down, far beyond the depth that would have taken us back to the ground floor.

It grew cooler, the skin on my exposed arms and upper torso growing goosebumps for the first time today. When the stairs ended, and the floor flattened out, we were well below the foundations of the house. The air had taken on that damp, musty smell I always associate with cellars.

I couldn't orientate myself – we could have been heading inland or directly for the cliff for all I knew. I marvelled at the existence of the passageway until I remembered that the family house was constructed to the specification of a man who had been a pirate. To such a person, a secret way in and out would have been second nature and with a jolt, I recalled Edward retelling the story of a ghostly attack on the house a century ago.

Or was it two centuries? I couldn't remember, but during the ride to his house last night, he had told me about his family's history and explained that they escaped harm by using an old smugglers' tunnel.

We were doing the same thing now.

If the people outside Edward's house had already stormed it looking for us, I could not tell. No sound followed us down the passageway which I took to be a positive sign.

Like Chinese whispers travelling back along the line of people ahead of me, a message arrived to say we had reached a set of stairs going back up. I peered around Tempest, the person immediately in front of me, but could not see the steps until I reached them.

Curious to discover where the passageway would exit, I found out soon enough when a shaft of light appeared ahead of and above me. Someone had opened a door to the outside.

I emerged a few seconds later, blinking in the dim, mist-filled sunlight and looking around to get my bearings. My friends were all around me – none of them had gone very far, and we were in the lee of a small stone building. I couldn't be sure in the mist, but I suspected we were still within the grounds of Edward's house.

"Is the mist beginning to clear?" hissed Martin. It sparked a hushed debate about whether visibility was going to improve soon or not. It was a good question, and Martin's assessment of the weather might have been right, but it was entirely secondary in my mind to what we should be doing now.

I gripped Tempest's sleeve, and then touched Jermaine's arm and pulled them and everyone else into a huddle.

"I think I have figured out what has been happening here and why Edward asked for our help," I announced once I had everyone's attention.

Gloria asked, "Does that mean you know where my grandson is?"

Her question forced me to admit, "Not exactly. But I think I know what happened to him and why there are so many people looking for Edward. We need to get back to Torruga, and we need to make contact with the mayor."

Barbie asked, "It's the chief of police, isn't it? He was running the scam, not Edward." She had read the same email as me and was checking what she believed to be the case.

I nodded. "I think so. How many of the police are involved I cannot say. What we do know is that we cannot call on local law enforcement to help us."

"But what can the mayor do?" asked Martin. "He doesn't have his own officers or a security force he can call upon."

He was one hundred percent right. Sort of. "No," I replied. "But he does have a direct line to the governor of the island, and he will be able to make contact with someone who can help."

With a frown, Alistair asked, "Who?"

23

BIG, BEEFY, AND BRITISH

It might be a little known fact, but any British territory, even one as small as the British Union Isles, has a military presence. Don't ask me how I know this, it's just one of those odd snippets of information one learns in life. I couldn't tell you where I was when I picked up this small piece of knowledge, or who it might have been that told me.

Regardless, somewhere on this island there were British troops. I doubted the mayor of a coastal resort had the authority to call upon them, but I was certain the governor did.

We had all the evidence we needed to bring the fraudulent land sale scam crashing down on Chief Quimby. I was certain that was what we had uncovered, and with the police after us and Sam still missing, the only thing we could do was expose the truth.

The mist provided cover, but it was beginning to lift. Whether we could get out of Edward's grounds without being spotted and find our way back to town was questionable. If the fog lifted completely and the police were on the look out for us, getting to the mayor's office, not that we knew where it was, would prove difficult.

Using Alistair's phone, I called the number he had for Angus.

"Mayor Boxley's office. Cynthia speaking. How may I direct

your call?" The voice that answered was that of an efficient sounding personal assistant. In her thirties perhaps, she was waiting to hear who I wanted to speak to.

Whispering because I didn't want to give my position away – the police were probably still at Edward's house and we were in the garden – I said, "Hello. This is Patricia Fisher …"

"Can you speak up, please," Cynthia asked politely.

"No, I can't," I hissed into the phone. "I need to speak to the mayor."

"I'm afraid the mayor is very busy. I can take your name and arrange an appointment." I heard her tapping keys on her keyboard. "He has an opening next Tuesday at half past three," she informed me, believing she was being helpful.

"No!" I hissed with all the urgency one can convey in a whisper. "It has to be now. I need to speak to him now. It is of the utmost importance."

"I'm sorry, madam. The only way I can help you is to arrange an appointment."

Okay, I get that I probably sounded like a crazy woman, whispering into the phone as I was, but if that was what Cynthia was thinking, I was about to make it a whole lot worse.

"Listen, Cynthia. I have evidence in my possession that shows the chief of Torruga police is involved in a scam to swindle money out of I don't know how many people. He has engaged in murder and kidnapping and is currently attempting to find me and my friends so he can stop us from bringing the truth to someone who can act on it."

Cynthia gasped, "Oh, my goodness."

"Get out of your chair, Cynthia. Get out of your chair and go directly to the mayor. Get him on the phone right now." My insistent demands had the desired effect, I could hear the staccato sound of her heels on a hard floor as she ran.

There was a brief and hurried exchange of words, Cynthia's voice being answered by an altogether deeper one. Then the mayor's voice was in my ear.

"Patricia? Is that you?"

I breathed a sigh of relief. "Angus, thank goodness. Angus we are in the grounds of Edward's house. Chief Quimby is behind a scam to defraud money out of anyone who has enough to invest. We are coming to you, but Chief Quimby is looking for us. His men cornered us at Edward's house."

Angus interrupted me to ask, "How did you get away?"

Dismissively, I shot back, "It's not important. We are in the grounds of Edward's house and about to leave. We'll need to take a circuitous route to avoid being spotted, but should be with you in less than an hour. I hope. I'll bring the evidence with me, but we need protection. Are there soldiers on the island?"

Quick as a flash, Angus replied with an answer that lifted my hopes. "Marines."

I knew it wouldn't be a large detachment, but a handful of heavily armed Royal Marine Commandos would be enough.

"Great. Can you get them to Torruga in the next hour?"

"I'll have to call the governor, but unless he argues, which I don't think he will, they are only twenty minutes away. Their base is just up the coast, and they have amphibious assault craft they can scramble."

More good news. I needed to end the call and get my team moving.

"Angus, I cannot thank you enough. I'm sure this comes as a terrible shock …" the back of my skull itched as I thought to question something.

"Patricia? Are you there?" The mayor's voice rumbled in my ear, returning me to the here and now.

"Yes. Sorry. I need to go. Please get the marines to Torruga as soon as you can and have them looking out for me and my motley crew. We'll be approaching from the high ground to the west of the town."

Angus confirmed that he understood my plan, wished me luck, and got off the phone – he had other calls to make.

"He's going to help?" asked Barbie the second I handed the phone back to Alistair.

To answer her, I said, "We just need to get what we have to him. The marines will be waiting for us."

"Really?" asked Molly, looking interested. "Like Royal Marines, you mean? Big, beefy British guys?"

Next to her, Pippin frowned. "Is there a shortage of men on board the Aurelia?"

To stop an argument developing – we really didn't have time for such nonsense. I stepped in between them.

"We have to go," I stated forcefully.

I could not have been more correct, it transpired, for shouting erupted from the direction of the house.

Chief Quimby's men had searched the house and whether they were guessing or not, they somehow knew we were on the grounds and were coordinating themselves to find us.

24

WATCH YOUR STEP

The sound of their quad bikes fired into life a few seconds later. I had frozen to the spot, but Jermaine grabbed my arm and yanked me after him as we all scarpered. Once again the mist provided us with the cover we needed to run away without being seen, but they were giving chase and getting back to the town had just got a whole lot harder.

I lost sight of everyone bar Jermaine almost immediately, the mist and the trees swallowing them up as they dispersed. I don't think any of us knew where we were going. The mission was to get to town, but that was in the opposite direction. At best we would have to take a wide circle to get around the police.

Just ahead to my left, I spotted Schneider with Gloria on his back. He was carrying her so she wouldn't get left behind.

The sound of my breathing filled my ears as I ran through the mist-laden garden. No one was shouting or saying anything at all; the only sounds from my friends were the crunch of a stick under someone's foot or the twang of a branch as they swept it to one side.

Alistair appeared at my side, his eyes showing his relief at finding me.

"We will have to go around them," he whispered the obvious.

The quad bikes chasing us were unable to follow as we delved deeper into the trees on this side of Edward's enormous garden. I wanted to orientate myself, but with no sun, no compass, and no visible landmarks, I was hopelessly lost. It was my first time in Edward's grounds, so even the bushes and trees we could see were of no help.

What trees?

Abruptly, like a bucket of cold water to my face, I noted that the trees, which had until a few seconds ago been pressing in close on either side, were now absent. With a jolt of blind panic, I dug in my heels and hit the brakes.

I had to fling out an arm to grab Alistair's sleeve and reverse Jermaine's grip on my arm so I was holding him instead.

Both men swung their heads inward. Questioning my sudden need to stop, they saw why as we came to a stop and the light breeze swirled the mist. In my head the trees around Edward's house continued into the distance in every direction bar one.

Alistair sucked in a sharp breath – we were less than three yards from the edge of the cliff. If we had continued running, we might not have noticed the land ending until we had run into free air.

Unhappy about giving away our position, but unwilling to risk one of my friends dying, I sucked in a deep breath and shouted a warning.

"We're at the cliff! Everyone watch out!"

The quad bikes, fifty yards or more behind us and going slow as they attempted to figure out where we might have gone, were instantly moving again.

Schneider crashed through the woods behind us. Gloria, hitched up high on his back, was picking bits of tree out of her hair and cursing. Along the way, they had collected Anders Pippin and Molly, who were holding hands to stay together.

Barbie, Deepa, Martin, and Hideki were nowhere in sight. Calling for them was probably foolhardy – Quimby's cops were already on their way to get us …

"Barbie!" I bellowed with all the volume I could muster.

Alistair put a finger to my lips and raised his right hand so it was in front of my face. In it he held a radio. Speaking at a more sensible volume, he called for Barbie to answer.

No reply came back from her, but Martin responded.

"I believe we are about twenty yards to your right. I heard Mrs Fisher yelling. I've got Deepa and Hideki with me."

Hideki's voice came over the airwaves, "Has anyone seen Barbie?" I could hear the concern in his voice. She was the fastest among us by quite some margin. If she had set off at a sprint, would she have seen the cliff before it was too late?

And where were Tempest and Big Ben? We had lost them too in the pea soup mist.

Unable to raise her with the radio, Hideki shouted her name, "Barbie!"

Alistair took my hand, speaking calmly into his radio, "Stay there. We're coming to you."

We made our way to them, going as fast as we could with the deadly cliff edge just a few yards to our left. All the while we listened to the sound of the quad bikes coming ever closer.

I wanted to find the missing members of our party. It wasn't just Sam now; Barbie and the Blue Moons were missing too. All three could take care of themselves, assuming they hadn't run off the cliff, but sticking together was not only far safer, but a good deal more comforting for me.

The quad bikes were still coming, however when we got to Martin, we discovered his group had found a path leading down the cliff. It was a trail of sorts, cut eons ago by nature and then enhanced and improved by man. Little more than a foot trail through the trees and shrubs clinging to the side of the island, we couldn't see how far it went, but one thing was clear – no quad bike was going to follow us down it.

Far too narrow for the motorised transport, and with no other options from which to pick, we set off.

Less than ten yards down the path, the roar of three or four quad bikes sounded above our heads. Having reached the cliff, they had either found our tracks or were imbued with sufficient local knowledge to know where we must have gone.

With my heart thumping inside my chest, I twisted around to look back to where we had just been. The start of the path was no longer visible – a small mercy, but the swirling mist might expose us at any second and it was definitely beginning to lift.

Urgent hands pulled me to one side and off the path, just as the engines above went to idle and shut off.

They were listening.

I was silent, holding my breath for fear that filling my lungs would give our position away. No one made a noise until an argument broke out above.

"They must have gone down there."

"Well, you go after them then," suggested a second voice in a mocking tone.

"What? I'm not going down there. That old path is deadly."

"Quimby wants them found," remarked a third voice.

They were all men, and all carried the same island accent.

The first voice replied, "Quimby wants them dead."

"Not all of them. They found a way to hide Edward Teach. We need to make sure the woman survives."

"Which woman? The blonde with the big …"

"No, not that one. The middle-aged one with the big bum."

I started to rise, drawing a breath as I thought to give them a piece of my mind.

Jermaine gripped my arm and whispered, "Perhaps now is not the time, madam."

The second voice spoke again, his tone as mocking as before. "So you go down there after them then. I'll say some kind things at your funeral."

I heard a crackle of radio, and Chief Quimby's voice coming over the airwaves.

"Status update. Report."

No one replied, the three men above us arguing about what they were going to do and who should respond to their boss.

"Report!" Quimby barked, jolting one of the men above to reply.

"They've taken the cliff path down to Balbon village, Sir. Chances are they won't make it …"

"Stop thinking, Evans!" Quimby raged, cutting the man off mid-sentence. "They know where Edward Teach is and he has the evidence. Or he said he had the evidence. For all we know they have it now. They must be eliminated, but we can't do that until we know for sure what they were able to find out. Leave one man there to make sure they don't come back up. The rest of you get back to the house. We will have to go after them on foot."

Evans wasn't happy. "Sir the old cliff path is completely eroded in places and crumbling in others. One wrong foot and it's a two-hundred-foot drop onto the rocks below."

Quimby's retort included an abundance of curse words, several accusations of cowardice, and reminder of what the consequences might be if the truth got out.

He ended his tirade with, "Just forget what I said earlier about shooting them on sight. I want all of them alive. Not just that Fisher woman."

The three quad bikers above us argued about who was going to stay, until the voice I knew to be Evans pulled rank. He picked one of the other two and told him, "If any of them come back up the path, shoot them."

"Quimby wants them alive," the one being left as sentry argued.

Evans replied in an exasperated tone. "So shoot them in the leg or the gut, idiot."

Two engines roared to life once more, the riders turning their quad bikes around and peeling away.

Carefully, and using touch and sign language rather than speech, we came back onto the path and slipped away.

We didn't go far though, just far enough that we were confident our voices wouldn't be heard by the sentry left behind. When the path rounded a corner to ensure we would be hidden if the mist shifted, we stopped and formed a gaggle to discuss our latest predicament.

Everyone was of a singular mind.

"They called the path deadly," said Deepa.

Molly was peering into the seaward mist. "I don't want to fall two hundred feet onto the rocks," she offered her opinion.

Alistair raised a point, "They also said it would take us to a village. We cannot go back up and we need to find a way to get back to Torruga. There will be boats at the village. We can pay someone for a quick ferry around the coast."

His point was valid, but not if we fell to our collective deaths before we got there.

A cry from above stopped the conversation dead in its tracks.

"I told you to not knock him out," moaned Tempest, my brain assuring me his comment had been aimed at Big Ben.

A soaring uplift of hope, something akin to euphoria, filled my soul. The Blue Moons were okay, and they had just dealt with the armed cop blocking us from going back up the cliff path.

Tempest called out, "Are you down there, Patricia?"

The decision to go back to them was made without the need for conversation - no one wanted to chance the cliff path.

Hideki came around me, keen to get back to the top. "Is Barbie up there?" he called through the mist.

Her voice when she replied had an edge to it. "Yeah, I'm here."

I found out what was bothering her when I got near to the top of the cliff path and could see her sitting on the ground. She was showing Hideki her left ankle – it was twice the size it ought to be.

She hadn't shot off ahead of us only to fall to her death when she reached the cliff, she'd twisted her ankle on an exposed tree root. Big Ben and Tempest had scooped her, but with the quad bikes so close to their position, they had gone to ground.

According to Tempest, movement is the thing that gives away a person's position faster than anything else. He started to explain about shadow, silhouette, shine, and some other stuff, but the point was, he and Big Ben knew from their army days that if they hugged the ground and stayed still, Quimby's men could walk right by without spotting they were there.

It also explained why Barbie hadn't answered her radio. She'd turned it off when the quad bikes came her way. Her ankle was a fat mess - she wasn't going to be running anywhere anytime soon, but we could manage.

Hideki would do what he could for her – I wanted to check how she was doing, but we just didn't have time. Quimby's men were going to be back soon. They would discover the sentry they left gone and if we were swift, it could give us all the advantage we needed.

25

HADEN FALLS

Big Ben was holding the unconscious sentry by one foot. Lifting him into the air so only his fingertips trailed on the grass, he asked, "What do I do with him?"

Tempest tutted. "Put him down, remove his weapons, cuff him using his own cuffs, and see if you can bring him around again."

Sounding like he was feeling put upon, Big Ben grumbled, "I only hit him once. It's not like I could have hit him fewer times."

"Yes," agreed Tempest, "but you could have punched him in the gut instead. He might have thrown up, but he would still be conscious for us to interrogate. I would very much like to know what is going on here."

"I think I've figured it out," I announced, checking the thoughts in my head again. "Probably. I need to make a couple of phone calls … when I've had a little more time to think things through, and I need to see how things play out now, but I believe I have it straight."

Barbie winced where Hideki was binding her ankle with one of his shirt sleeves.

"Okay, Patty, spill," she demanded.

Alistair spoke before I could. "No time. We need to get moving. They will be back soon enough." He pointed to the unconscious sentry who Big Ben had now disarmed and cuffed. "Let's put a gag on him and drop him off somewhere out of sight. Barbie and Gloria can ride on the quad bike, the rest of us can run behind."

There was no need to suggest a counter proposal – his plan was sound. The hard part was going to be getting around the cops to make our way back to Torruga.

Tempest volunteered his thoughts while Hideki and Martin helped Barbie onto the quad bike.

"We heard what they said – they think you are on the cliff path, but we must assume they are wise enough to leave the route back to Torruga covered. If we take it, they will catch us. We need to go around."

Jermaine produced the ordnance survey map we'd found at Edward's house, folding it out so we could look at it. The scale was not such that we could use it to find a safe route back to the town, but it was good enough to show me something.

I jabbed a finger at the map. "That's Haden Falls!" On the map it just looked like a lake, but I remembered where it was from the ship's online excursions brochure.

Alistair clicked his fingers and kissed my head. "Well done, darling."

Tempest didn't understand the significance.

"Um, what's at Haden Falls?"

Martin answered, "Horses. Lots and lots of horses."

Barbie was on the quad bike with Gloria holding on tight to her waist. The grimace of pain from her twisted ankle was there in her eyes, but she was going to fight it. She pulled away, the rest of us falling into a jog behind her.

We judged it was perhaps two miles to Haden Falls, a fifteen to twenty minute run we hoped. I was the least fit of anyone present so it was my pace that would determine when we got there, but our destination took us in what we hoped was a completely unpredictable direction.

If Quimby and his men managed to figure out we were not on the cliff path, they would never think to check the route to Haden Falls.

Or so I hoped.

On the way, huffing and already out of breath, I tried to explain to Tempest why there would be horses at Haden Falls. Hearing my laboured breathing, Jermaine took over.

"It is one of the most popular passenger destinations," he explained. "The falls are a natural phenomenon, fresh water from the mountains dropping over a hundred feet into a pool with naturally shallow beaches to either side. There are groups of passengers setting off to get there every hour during daylight."

"They don't have the best day for it," remarked Alistair, breathing hard from the effort of running himself. "In the sun, the Falls are spectacular."

I had wanted to see the Falls myself. It was on our list of things to do during our brief visit to the island. Given how badly things had gone since the moment we set foot on land, I should be thankful I was getting to visit the tourist attraction at all.

Thankful I had worn sensible shoes for the day knowing how likely it was that I would end up running, I still wanted to stop and take a breather. I was drenched with a combination of sweat and the penetrating dampness from the mist that continued to grow thinner. Looking up now, we could see the sun beating down even though it was like looking at it through a layer of gauze.

The yards became miles and the mist continued to thin. We were thankful for it, and for Tempest's ability to read the topography of the land. He was eyeballing it, doing his best to get us to where we needed to go without a compass.

Barbie was sent to scout ahead a few times, the radios ensuring we never lost them.

Just shy of twenty-five minutes later, uncertainty of route through woodland adding at least half a mile, we heard Barbie's whoop over the radio.

"I can hear people! I think we found it." Quiet followed as we slowed to walking a pace and listened for Barbie's confirmation. "I see it! There are dozens of horses!"

Less than a minute later, we saw them too. Haden Falls, a stunning natural landmark was right there for us to explore and enjoy, but we were not going to get the chance to do so. We were coming up on twenty hours into a twenty-four-hour visit. We needed to finish up the awful case we found ourselves mixed up in, get Sam back, and return to the ship.

I had been so excited to explore this island paradise, but all I wanted now was a gin and tonic in the security of my suite.

We caught up to Barbie, who was watching the horses through the trees. Beyond them, passengers from the ship were frolicking in the natural lake and enjoying food and drinks from the restaurant set up near the shore to cater to them.

Tending the horses were two young women. Both in their early thirties, they bore the tanned skin all islanders display. The horses were saddled and ready to go, all of them tethered to a fence where they were happily munching on piles of hay dropped there for them.

We needed a distraction.

Big Ben said, "I guess that's my cue," and pulled off his top.

Molly said, "Wow."

I'd seen Big Ben's ridiculously lean and muscular torso before, but I had to admit it was worth looking at again. Deepa was trying not to look though Martin caught her surreptitious glances.

Hideki, lean and muscular himself though on a completely different scale – Big Ben was mostly off the scale – frowned with disapproval.

Pumping his arms and then giving his biceps a hard slap to make the veins pop, Tempest's colleague strolled around to our right, taking a circuitous route to get to the ladies so they would be looking his way and not ours when they spotted him.

We were going to sneak in to grab a horse each once he had their attention.

"I'll need a few minutes," Big Ben announced. "Maybe ten to fifteen if they are both willing."

Deepa blinked. "I'm sorry? Willing? He's planning to have sex with them?"

Molly murmured something that sounded a lot like she was

volunteering her name for the list. I placed a hand on her head and steered her toward the horses.

We watched, peering through the trees as the topless hunk waved a hello to get the ladies' attention and then proceeded to flirt with them. I didn't think he was serious about doing anything else, but we never got to find out, because that was when Quimby sprung his trap.

26

HORSE THIEVES

The sound of a dozen or more quad bikes started as a faint noise in the background. A bit like when you have a mosquito in your bedroom at night, the faint whine was enough to distract us, but not enough to focus our attention until we realised it was coming closer.

The arc of approach took in about sixty degrees, the quad bikes fanned out behind us as they charged toward the lake. How they had tracked us became apparent a moment later when Quimby's voice came over our radios.

"Surrender now. You will all be given a fair trial."

We knew that wasn't true. We all heard him tell Evans that we had to be silenced. We'd been communicating with Barbie as she scouted the route ahead with Gloria on the quad bike and he'd found the channel we were talking over. We had led him right to Haden Falls.

The quad bikes were closing in and the girls minding the horses had heard them. Their attention was no longer on Big Ben who was trying to get their focus back by making his pectoral muscles dance up and down.

The chance to sneakily grab the horses was already lost. Completely so when Tempest shouted, "Grab a nag and let's go!"

We charged forward, running to get to the line of horses. Some of them were lifting their heads, looking around lazily to see who was disturbing their down time.

The ladies saw what we were doing, screaming an alarm that alerted more of their colleagues. Now we had the cops closing in behind and the equestrian workers running at us from the lake! Alistair leapt onto a horse, throwing a leg up and landing on its back as if he'd been born in the saddle. To my left and right, Deepa, Martin, Schneider, heck even Molly were on their horses and moving.

If I didn't get my horse moving in the next few seconds, I was going to get caught. However, where everyone else seemed to just stick a foot in a stirrup and leap into the air, my horse kept moving. I couldn't seem to coordinate my movements, and every time I flung myself skyward the horse shifted and I landed back on the ground again.

Obviously, because it's me, on what had to be my fifth or sixth attempt, I landed awkwardly with one foot and lost my balance. I fell backward, arms pinwheeling and came to land with my face just a few inches from something the horse's back end had ejected.

Alistair saw my plight, turning his horse around to come back for me.

I tried to get up, but my stupid foot was caught in the stirrup. I had to get that free first, but the rotten horse kept moving. I was crunching my abs to get to my foot and grunting from the effort. All the while the horse – I swear it was doing it on purpose - was dragging me closer to the pile of poop. Looking through the horse's legs as I fought to get away from the horrible, steaming heap on the ground by my head, I spotted the quad bikes. They were flying through the woods, their arrival mere seconds away now.

They were not, however, the more immediate threat even if they were the more dangerous one – the equestrian team was closer.

They were however not, it transpired, closest.

Demonstrating how fast long muscular legs can go, Big Ben had outrun the two women he went to distract. I thought he was going to pick me up, but instead he smacked my horse on the bum and yelled at it.

"Hhyyyyyaah!"

Shocked, my horse reared onto its back legs and then took off. Meanwhile Big Ben had swung himself onto another horse and was chasing after me.

Now, how can I put this politely? I'm not sure I can find the words. I was being dragged along the ground by a horse. I've seen such stunts performed by men in old westerns and the like, but they wore leather chaps for the task, not a cheap, thin pirate costume that was basically a dress. Whizzing forward with one foot still stuck in a stirrup, I was surfing the earth on my bottom with my legs acting as a funnel for the twigs, sticks, and what at one point felt like a hedgehog, that littered the ground.

Universally, they were heading for a part of me I wanted very few things to ever go, and I couldn't figure out how to improve my situation. Certainly, screaming enough curse words to make me self-combust if I were in church wasn't helping.

It was a mercy that there was leaf litter for me to skid over or I might have lost a lot more skin than I did.

I thought I had gone a mile, but when Big Ben caught up to my horse and reigned it in, I had only travelled about twenty-five yards. Alistair was there to help extract me from the tangle of undergrowth I'd collected.

I could have clambered onto my horse at this point, but it felt likely to just end in my death somewhere farther down the trail, so I grabbed Alistair's hand and climbed up behind him instead.

A whip-crack reverberated between the trees – the cops were shooting at us.

"Surrender now!" ordered Quimby, but his instructions were pointless. We were running for our lives now and the question came down to whether the horses they used for the slow tourist jaunts through the woods would be able to outrun some quad bikes.

It was time to find out.

Big Ben yelled again to get his horse moving; mine had spotted some wild grass and had gone back to grazing, and we were off.

Bullets followed us through the woodland, but incredibly the horses outpaced the quad bikes in no time at all. It was as if the old dobbins, for that was what they looked like to me, had finally been given an opportunity to run after years of traipsing everywhere at a boring pace, and were taking full advantage.

We were horse thieves, but I believe we would be forgiven when the truth came out. All we had to do now was beat Quimby back to Torruga.

That was going to be easy enough and we even had a trail to follow this time because the horses had clearly been following the same one for years. I doubted, though, that it would be as easy as that and of course it wasn't.

Our route swept back down through the mountains toward the coast and before long we began to catch glimpses of the sea and then of Torruga itself. I could pick out the white of the cathedral and the red roofs of the houses surrounding it …

I gasped. "The mist. It's gone!"

Where it lingered still, caught in the cooler temperature beneath the canopy the trees formed, there was no trace of it in the open. It gave for a wonderful view of the Aurelia, sitting majestically against a backdrop of sparkling blue ocean. With our elevation and the uninterrupted view, we could see the curvature of the earth as it met the horizon.

We could also see the waiting police blockade stretched out across the route into Torruga.

"Are you seeing this?" asked Tempest, bringing his horse alongside mine.

I nodded.

Alistair leaned his head to one side so he could look back at me. "That's not going to be easy to get around."

He wasn't wrong. I looked behind us and listened, but we hadn't heard the quad bikes in a couple of minutes and if they were still pursuing us, we would hear them coming long before they were able to spot us.

I tapped Alistair's shoulder. "I need your phone, sweetie."

"You're going to call the mayor?" he sought to confirm.

My skull itched. I'd missed something. I'd missed something important. I'd missed something that would have gotten us all killed if I hadn't just spotted the glaring error in my theory.

The distant buzz of a quadbike engine reached my ears. Our pursuers were coming.

"I need to split us up," I announced, my words instantly met with argument. "I've been wrong about who is involved and why." My admission stilled most of their comments. "Our way into Torruga is blocked, and I'm betting they have similar blockades on every street we might choose to use. The only way to end this is to get the truth to the one man who can do something with it. The mayor called the marines, but that's no good to us if we cannot get to him."

Barbie asked, "Can't they come to us? A heavily armed escort can walk us through the town."

It was a valid suggestion and something I had considered myself.

However, I told the group, "I don't think they can. I don't know how many of them there are, but even if it is fifty or a hundred and fifty, I think Quimby will try to kill us anyway. He thinks we have evidence that will convict him, plus we would have to find somewhere to hide and have them come to us. We already know we can't use the radios because they are listening. The quadbikes closing in behind us will push us toward town." Everyone was listening, and though they didn't like it, they all accepted that I was probably right. Now they were primed to hear my plan, I said, "Here's what I think we should do."

27

CHESS PIECES

Alistair was not happy about being split from me – he wanted me at his side, but I had a task for him that no one else could do. He went with Martin and Deepa, the three planning to ditch their horses when they got close to town. They were dressed like tourists out for the day and would switch into pirate gear the moment they found a place selling some.

Dressed either way, they would blend in and Quimby's men were looking for a big group of us, not a trio of individuals.

Tempest and Big Ben had a different task. They wished me luck and set off on foot. The edge of the town was a mile down the mountain from where we were, and the coastline another mile and a half beyond that. They were going to have to make fast time – the success of the whole thing was contingent on several factors and their task was one of them.

Jermaine stayed with me – I wouldn't have been able to convince him otherwise anyway. Molly and Pippin stayed too, the four of us planning to ride our horses around the outskirts of the town. I had a destination in mind that was most likely best accessed by coming in from the north. It would be a slog to get there, but that would give the others time to do what they needed to achieve and would once again defy Quimby's expectations. Far from heading toward the town, we were heading away from it. At least to start with.

That just left Barbie, Hideki, and Gloria. Barbie couldn't walk, not without support, and Gloria was, as she put it, 'cream crackered'. Her colloquial phrase was lost on all but the British in our group who knew the cockney rhyming slang for knackered just meant she was too tired to do anything more today.

They were heading directly for the ship, once again relying on the reduced size of their party to get them through. If they struggled, they would lie low and wait for the police to disperse. That was going to happen soon enough I assured them. Their biggest challenge was going to be getting Barbie through the town once they ditched the quad bike. They had no choice but to do so, it was marked up with police livery and would be spotted in seconds.

With everyone heading off in different directions, my party coaxed our horses into action again. Even though we had horses to spare, I was riding behind Jermaine now, feeling far safer clinging to him than I would have done on a horse of my own.

I had copied the mayor's number from Alistair's phone into mine, but I waited nearly an hour before I called him. By then I had received confirmation from other members of our team that their tasks were in hand. We had taken our lengthy route around the town and were coming down onto the beach at the far northern edge. There was nothing here – it was way beyond the outer edge of the town, and the slope, while negotiable on horseback, was too steep for anyone to build on.

Expecting Cynthia again, I was surprised when Angus's voice came on the line, "Mayor Boxley."

"Angus, it's Patricia."

"Patricia! Thank goodness! Are you all right? Where are you now? There have been reports from some tourist groups by Haden Falls about shots being fired. I worried that might have been something to do with you?"

I waited for his salvo of questions to die down before speaking, but didn't bother to supply him with answers.

"There needs to be a change of plans, Angus. I am not going to be able to get to your office – Quimby's men are blocking the route."

"You're kidding!" he spat. "The brazenness of the man! What do you need, Patricia? Where can I meet you? I'll come to you, and you can share with me all the information you have. I will make sure Quimby gets what he deserves."

I thanked Angus for his help, and for his fortitude in taking on his own chief of police.

"We are just approaching the docks, Angus. I expect Quimby has men positioned to stop us getting back to the Aurelia though. Can you meet us at pier twelve?" I asked, reading the sign painted on the large, covered boatshed to my front.

"How soon?"

"I'm just arriving there now."

Angus promised to make all haste but to also take great care to make sure he wasn't seen or followed. As part of the festivities, he was already fully decked out in pirate garb, and with a little makeup and a few changes to his costume, believed he could pass by Chief Quimby's men without being identified.

This would all be done far better at night in the dark when shadows would afford greater opportunity to sneak about, but I wasn't inclined to wait. It was coming up on twenty-four hours since I'd last seen Sam and I wanted him back at my side.

The call complete, I then used my phone's internet search function to find a listing for Strawberry Moons Nightclub and thumbed the button to connect us.

When a polite young man answered the phone, I said, "Hello, this is Patricia Fisher. I'm responsible for breaking into Tommy DeMeco's office today. Please tell him I have Edward Teach with me and we are heading to Pier Twelve at the docks. I'll hold while you connect me."

The young man did not sound like he was one of DeMeco's hoodlums and was most likely part of the legitimate business of the nightclub. My demands flustered him, but he put me through. After just a few seconds, I heard Tommy's voice in my ear.

"Well, well, well," he remarked in his rough cockney accent. "I thought I was going to have to chase you. It's not like I could let you get away with the little stunt you pulled off today."

"Save it, DeMeco," I snapped. "I have Edward Teach and you want your money back. Why don't you tell me how much it is, and I will have it waiting for you?"

Tommy didn't answer immediately, the delay nothing more than the petty gangster trying to decide what he wanted more – the money or to repay me for my insults.

When he finally responded, he growled, "He owes me five million US. You owe me the same, understand? Ten million and I will let you walk away. That's my price."

"I will have it waiting." I ended the call without feeling the need for pleasantries. I didn't have ten million, and though I was sure a call to the Maharaja's people would have that amount sitting in an account of my choosing within minutes, I was not going to give Tommy DeMeco a penny. He was a local criminal, and though not involved in the scam that had caused my nightmarish time on this island, he was nevertheless a cockroach who needed to be stepped on.

When the beach reached the docks, Jermaine pulled on the reins to stop the horse. Molly and Pippin did likewise, all four of us dismounting to walk the final hundred or so yards to the boatshed. The place where Davy and his friends had been fishing earlier was now taken up by kids who were launching themselves off the dock and into the waves over and over again with gleeful abandon. I wondered how many generations had done the same.

Jermaine offered them US dollars – twenty bucks apiece, the notes nice and shiny – to walk the horses back to the stables. The kids knew where that was and set off riding in ones and twos arguing about who got to hold the reins.

I watched them for a moment, allowing myself to forget about the nightmarish day I'd been forced to endure. Their careless joy was just so out of place in contrast to the inner turmoil I felt. I believed I knew what had happened to Sam, but it was all just a theory until I could get to the man behind his disappearance and find out if I was right.

"Madam," Jermaine prompted. He didn't need to say any more. I had positioned all the chess pieces and now it was time to strike.

Molly and Pippin had reached the boatshed and were peering through a pedestrian door. There was a large roller door dominating the side facing inland and I knew the shed would be open and exposed on the opposite side facing out to sea.

That it was empty of the people working there and left unlocked for me to enter was another thing I had hastily arranged to happen.

With my arm latched onto Jermaine's crooked elbow, we made our way to the building set at the far end of the docks. It was far enough away from the Aurelia and the passengers coming and going from it, and from the other people working in and around the dockyard. Molly and Pippin were inside and had found hiding places by the time I went through the door Jermaine held open for me.

They were nowhere in sight, and I did not call for them.

Jermaine had the maps and other pieces of evidence tucked under one arm. Whether we needed them or not was entirely moot; they looked like evidence and that was the important thing.

I continued on through the boat yard, passing under a large crane used for lifting yachts from the water and onward until I reached the leading edge of the concrete platform. I stopped where it met the water and turned around to face back toward the door.

Angus arrived just a few minutes later.

28

WHO ARE THE REAL CRIMINALS?

The mayor of Torruga spotted me the moment he came through the door. I was standing with Jermaine, my rock by my side for moral support as well as for protection.

"Patricia," Angus called out. "I'm so glad to see you again. And I'm so sorry for what has happened during your visit to our peaceful island. I tried to quiz Chief Quimby about what was happening before lunch, but all I got were evasive answers and a promise to debrief me fully once he was able to get to the bottom of the events surrounding Edward Teach's disappearance. Have you been able to locate him?"

While talking, he had crossed the boatshed and now he was with us, his eyes were focussed on the maps and pieces of paper clutched in Jermaine's hands.

"Edward Teach," Angus repeated. "Do you know where he is? Is he safe?"

I bowed my head. "No, Angus. Both Edward and my friend, Sam, are still missing, their whereabouts unknown."

The mayor of Torruga made suitable sounds of disappointment.

"Well, perhaps no news is good news, eh?" He pointed to the

stash of evidence held in Jermaine's arms. "This is what you were able to find?"

"I thought you were coming with the Royal Marines," I pointed out.

Angus pulled a sorry face. "They are engaged in an exercise on the other side of the island. I spoke with their commander, and he said they would make best speed, but the earliest he estimated they could possibly get here is another three hours from now. Does it matter though?" he questioned. "Once I have the evidence securely locked away, I can move on the chief of police once the marines arrive."

"Well then," I invited Angus forward to see what we had. "You'd better take a look."

"Where did you find all this?" he asked, taking the refolded ordnance survey map from Jermaine.

"We found a secret office. Everything was there," I reported.

Angus shook his head. "A secret office. Goodness."

"That's right," I confirmed. Angus's attention was on the material Jermaine held. He opened the map. "What is this?" he asked, inspecting the area of the map where the runway and airport were superimposed.

I leaned over to point to the land where the runway ended and the name 'Teach's Reach'.

"An offshore airport, Angus. Chief Quimby devised an elaborate scam to sucker the rich into investing their money. They were being sold worthless land along the shore with the belief that were the airport proposal to go ahead, the land would instantly be worth millions."

Angus gawped at me. "I dare say it would. But it's all fake, you say?"

"Indeed. Chief Quimby must have approached Edward at some point, assuming one of the most famous islanders would have cash to invest in such a golden opportunity."

Angus nodded along, taking another piece of paper from Jermaine to inspect it.

"That makes sense. So this is all about money, then?"

"It often is," I sighed. "Unfortunately for Chief Quimby, Edward didn't have the money to invest. So far as I can work out, he's flat broke."

Angus hitched an eyebrow at me, a frown forming for the first time.

I continued to explain what I had bene able to figure out, "Edward hasn't been paying his staff and they have all quit. The most recent one went just over a week ago when Tommy DeMeco visited his house. Do you know what he was there for?" I asked, teasing Angus along.

Angus looked baffled and also a little impatient like he had somewhere else he needed to be.

"I couldn't possibly guess," he replied with a shrug.

I pursed my lips and nodded, taking a moment to select what I wanted to say next.

"Edward didn't have the money and the bank wouldn't lend him any. You might think taking a loan out against his house and estate would have been the sensible option, but I think Edward is far more broke than anyone realises. I don't think he even owns the house now, bad debts have stacked up and it's only a matter of time before the bank takes it from him."

To my mind this ought to have shocked the mayor, but I got so little reaction from him that he had to have already known.

"Edward borrowed the money from Tommy DeMeco," I supplied the answer to my own unspoken question.

Angus got to the back of the pile of paper Jermaine held and found the portable data drive resting in Jermaine's palm.

"This is a copy of everything on Edward's computer," Jermaine remarked, handing it over.

Angus's eyes lit up. "The secret computer in the secret office that no one knew about, you mean," he cradled the tiny data file. "This is everything then? Everything you were able to find?"

I nodded, showing my relief that I was able to now pass it on. "Yes."

Angus took a step back and lifted his right arm to his face.

Speaking into the cuff of his thin summer jacket, he said, "I have it all. You can come in now."

The door to the boatshed burst open, Chief Quimby leading the way as two dozen cops filed in behind him. They were all armed, not that any of them had their weapons drawn – they saw no need. They were facing down two unarmed civilians and they didn't want to kill them here where it might be heard. They would if they had to, but the plan was most likely to make us disappear forever, our bodies never to be discovered.

Angus had turned around to watch Chief Quimby make his way across the boatshed, so was talking over his shoulder when he said, "It's a shame, Patricia, that you had to poke your nose in. I told you to leave it alone and you were given the opportunity to do so. I know you feel you needed to find your friend, but honestly, we don't have him." Comment delivered, his admission of guilt now in the open, he rotated back to face me.

Only then did he see the smile on my face.

"Peter Webster." I said the name and fell silent, watching the mayor to see how he reacted.

He twitched one eyebrow, attempting to decipher what I meant.

"There were several things I could not work out. Not to start with, Angus." His eyebrows pinched together, his expression a mixture of curiosity and mild interest. "Edward said he believed his life was in danger. Actually, I think it was one of the only honest things he said, but like a friend of mine would say: once a pirate, always a pirate. His life was in danger, wasn't it? He figured out you had scammed him, and he wanted his money back. You refused and he threatened to expose it all."

"It wasn't a scam," Angus' frown deepened. "That's a deplorable word. It was a genuine investment opportunity. What if someone does decide to build an offshore runway? I would be in a position to steer them toward where it would be sited."

"No, you wouldn't" I argued. "Even if such a feat of engineering were possible, which I doubt very much it is, then the people building it would site it where it made sense, not where some fool politician wanted it."

Angus shrugged. "Perhaps. How did you figure out I was involved?" This was the question he wanted me to answer. He believed he had been so clever.

"It started with Peter Webster," I said the man's name again. "The involvement of Tommy DeMeco surprised me until I figured out that Edward didn't have any money with which he could invest. He borrowed it from Tommy DeMeco and when he told the loan shark criminal that he couldn't repay him, Tommy chose to give Edward some additional incentive."

"Incentive?" Angus didn't understand what I meant.

Chief Quimby arrived by his side, his men fanning to form a loose semi-circle around me and Jermaine.

"What are we doing, Angus," Chief Quimby asked. "Let's get them and get out of here. This has taken up enough time and effort already."

The mayor of Torruga shot out an arm to stop the chief of police from advancing toward me.

"No, I want to hear what she has to say. There have been mistakes. She knows more than I would have thought possible. We need to plug the gaps and we still don't know where Edward is."

"Ah, yes," I took his point and ran with it. "Everyone wants Edward. He was missing, but none of the interested parties had him. That confused me too."

"Who cares?" snapped Quimby, attempting to barge past the mayor. "You can take your confusion to the grave. After you have told me where Edward Teach is. I'm not stupid enough to believe your lies. You were there with him last night and no one has seen him since."

Angus shouted, "No!"

It was enough to stop Chief Quimby in his tracks.

"No? You want to say 'No' Angus?"

"That's Mayor Boxley," Angus growled. "This was all my idea, remember? You and your men are getting rich and have jobs for life because of me."

"Precisely," I joined in their conversation. "That was another thing that bothered me. Chief Quimby couldn't sell this investment.

No offense intended," I assured the chief of police. "What I mean is, the police chief is not the right person to present multi-millionaires with an investment opportunity. How would you in your work come into a situation where you knew about a proposed offshore airport?"

Angus sniggered a wry laugh at himself. "So you figured it out because it had to be someone charismatic, like me."

Quimby's eyes popped out. "I can be charismatic. I'm thoroughly charming, in fact."

Dismissing him, Angus asked, "What were you saying about Peter Webster?"

Picking up sort of where I left off, I said, "I found Peter at Strawberry Moons Nightclub earlier today. You revealed last night that one of your accountants had gone missing. That was Peter, wasn't it. He was being … incentivised," I deliberately chose the same word I'd used for Edward's interaction with Tommy DeMeco. "Edward had a limp, the result, I'm fairly sure of Mr DeMeco inflicting injuries intended to make Edward find a way to repay his money. Edward couldn't, and motivated by pain, he told Tommy all about how he'd been duped and how it was that you now had his money."

"That's right!" remarked Tommy DeMeco, coming through the boatshed with thirty of his lieutenants. Apart from Jermaine, I was the only one in the place facing the door and had seen him arrive. "You got my money, Boxley, and I want it back."

The police, responding to the new threat, went to draw their weapons, but the gangsters had the drop on them.

"Uh, uh, uh," Tommy held a machine pistol in his right hand and was wagging a finger with his left. "Don't be doing anything silly now, gentlemen. I already have a low tolerance for cops. If I'd known you all were dirty, we could have been in business. Right now, all I want is my money back." He winked at me. "And your money too, sweetheart. I hope you have it with you."

Chief Quimby wasn't about to be intimidated. "You cannot hope to get away with this, DeMeco. If you harm any of my officers …"

Tommy twitched his gun to the left and fired off a shot. With a yelp, one of the cops fell to the ground, clutching his leg where he had a new hole. The gun came back to point at Chief Quimby.

"You were saying?" Tommy taunted him.

I didn't know if the chief of police was going to challenge DeMeco again, and I wasn't going to give him the chance. If I was right, I wasn't getting Sam back until this was over, which meant it was time to wrap things up.

"You're planning to kill us?" I asked.

Angus looked from me to Tommy, to Chief Quimby, and then back to me.

With a shrug, the mayor of Torruga said, "Yes."

"Then will you indulge me by answering a few questions."

Chief Quimby acted like he couldn't believe his ears. "What is this nonsense? This isn't a movie, Angus. The bad guys don't reveal their plans when they have no reason to do so."

Tommy shot another cop in the leg. He did it just to get attention. "Hey, no one kills her until I get my money, okay? She's got ten million for me. Unless you two are actually going to stump up Edward's five million."

No one argued, so after a moment, I started talking again. "You killed the original landowner when he wouldn't sell you the land. Is that right?"

"Goodness, no, Patricia." Angus looked horrified by my suggestion. "I had Chief Quimby do it."

The chief of police growled, "Stop telling her what we did."

Tommy argued, "No, I like this. Keep asking questions. Who knew the mayor and the chief of police were the real crooks in this town? I feel like I need to up my game." His comment was met with laughter from his men and from two of the cops who thought it was funny until they saw none of their colleagues were laughing.

"Then using your influence as mayor, you arranged to buy the land," I continued. "That's what set this all into motion, right? You saw an opportunity to get rich and you didn't care who it hurt."

"Oh, this is so much more than a chance to get rich, Patricia. I already have all the money I'll ever need. This is about power.

Thousands of islanders have been 'selected' to be a part of this amazing opportunity. They don't have the money to invest, but they have collateral of another kind – their houses. They sign over the deeds to me as a retainer to be returned when the portion of the land they own at Teach's Reach achieves its full potential."

"Which it never will," I concluded.

"Which it never will," Angus repeated my statement. "But what can they do? They chose to invest. No one forced them to do it. They will learn the firm I invented for this venture chose to postpone the project, but that's not the same as cancelled. They just need to hang on and the plan to make them superrich might yet come to fruition. I can keep them dangling on that hook for at least a decade, and what can they do? They can't ask for their money back. They can't complain. Who would they complain to? I'm the mayor." He explained his plan with a cruel laugh. "I'm sorry, Patricia, but if you brought Mr DeMeco here to disrupt things, all you have done is introduce me to a new business partner."

The muzzle of Tommy's machine gun lowered a few inches, and he spoke to the men around him.

"You hear that, boys? We're going up in the world."

Satisfied with Tommy's answer, Angus turned around to look at me again.

"Anything else, Patricia? Any more questions? I'm afraid I lied about calling the governor. The Royal Marines are not coming to rescue you. No one is."

"How sure are you?" asked Tempest Michaels, stepping out from behind a piece of machinery thirty yards to my right.

His sudden appearance startled everyone in the boatshed, a small arsenal of guns swinging around to point in his direction. A volley of shots rang out, but they hit empty air as Tempest ducked back out of sight.

"I know you didn't call the governor," I let Angus know as I took a step back. I was holding Jermaine's hand as tightly as I could.

Tommy sent a dozen of his men to look for Tempest, and that was where everyone was looking. Everyone but Angus, who had heard my claim and was slowly twisting around because he had worked out what I was going to say next.

With a grin, I said, "Because I did."

From the water outside the open end of the boatshed, a thunder of throttles being cranked to fully open filled the air. Eyes turned that way, but just as they did, all around the boatshed the security team from the Aurelia popped out from their hiding places. The combined forces of Tommy's poorly trained hoodlums and the local cops whose weapons were still holstered, added up to less than fifty.

They were staring at more than three hundred guns.

Gripping Jermaine's hand, I stepped backward off the concrete and held my breath as I plunged into the water.

The roar of engines outside changed in both tone and volume as the Royal Marines rocketed into the boatshed. They were riding low on-board ribs that flew across the water at a speed intended to strike fear into anyone foolish enough to stand against them.

Spinning in all directions as they looked for a direction in which they could run, the cops and gangsters in the middle of the boatshed were getting screamed at from every angle.

From my position of relative safety in the water, I dared to pop my head up just far enough to see what happened to the group who went after Tempest.

Separated from the rest, those dozen men had frozen like everyone else when the Aurelia's crew popped into sight and the Royal Marines so abruptly charged to my rescue.

Swarmed by the Aurelia's security team, ably led by Alistair, they were already laying down their arms.

The fight was over before it even started, the combined shock tactics and mass of numbers was enough to prevent even the most foolhardy from thinking they might be able to shoot their way out.

Jermaine insisted I be helped from the water first, two Royal Marines lifting me into the air before depositing me back on the concrete. I thanked them and looked around, waiting for Jermaine to join me.

Alistair was easy to pick out. He was bedecked in his captain's uniform, the tropical one with the shorts and the short-sleeved shirt.

I liked how it showed off his muscular arms and legs. My plan to lure the mayor and everyone else back to the quayside had met with his approval due to a very simple fact: Inside the dock area his officers are permitted to carry their weapons and, if necessary, employ them if it can be proven the ship or a passenger is in danger.

This situation had counted.

Tempest and Big Ben were making their way over to me, but had to weave through a bunch of the Aurelia's security team. Big Ben made it as far as the first gaggle of women and stopped to chat with them. I'd asked the Blue Moon boys to find the Royal Marines. They had been in a different service at a different time, but Tempest had assured me they could prove who they were and deliver them when they were needed.

Clearly, it had not been hyperbole, though I hadn't known that for sure until we arrived in the boatshed, and I got the nod from Tempest to tell me everything was in place.

Alistair detached himself from the Royal Marines' commander with whom he had been speaking and jogged across to check on me.

"Darling you were magnificent," he praised me. I didn't argue. "Do you need a blanket to keep you warm?"

"We're on the equator, sweetie. The water isn't even all that cold." It had surprised me how warm it was when I went in, given that it was the Atlantic.

"A drink?" he offered. "I can get a steward here with a gin and tonic in under five minutes."

I couldn't help but laugh. Alistair Huntley, captain of an entire cruise ship, was fussing around me to the detriment of everyone else and desperately trying to be of use to me. I reached up to grab his chin and pulled him into a kiss.

All around us, Royal Marines, Alistair's crew, and even the criminals on their knees in organised lines, looked away.

When our lips parted, Alistair asked, "How did you know the mayor wasn't going to call the governor?"

29

THE BIG REVEAL

"It was when we met Peter Webster," I admitted. "I didn't connect the dots at the time, but later when I remembered the mayor pestering Chief Quimby about his missing accountant, I realised that was who we found in Tommy DeMeco's office. It made me curious about how all the pieces went together. The same gangster who was visiting Edward was also kidnapping the mayor's accountant? It was too much coincidence."

We had left the boatshed and were walking back along the dock to the Aurelia. Barbie, in a wheelchair that she wasn't very happy about, had insisted Hideki bring her to meet us.

"There must be more to it than that, Patty," she insisted, squinting her eyes at me in defiance because I so often refuse to give up my secrets.

I chuckled, and said, "When I called Angus to tell him about the evidence we had found, he wasn't in the least bit surprised. Then, when I told him where we were, Chief Quimby's cops came after us only seconds after our call ended."

Molly gasped. "That rat told them where to find us."

Barbie wasn't finished with her questions. "What will happen to the police?" she wanted to know. "Who's going to arrest them and charge them? Are there any other police on the island?"

I only knew the answer because I'd posed the same question to the governor.

"There are other police, but they all work for Quimby. The governor cannot be sure how far the corruption goes so he is suspending all the officers that were not there today until a full enquiry can exonerate or condemn them. To get around his problem, he is reinstating a few retired officers he believes can be trusted, including one former chief of police – he's eighty-three," I revealed, "and he has asked for a contingent of police to be sent over from Great Britain – sort of a busman's holiday, if you like." The governor was hoping some of them might be convinced to stay long term and move their families out to join them.

The sun was dipping toward the horizon and the day was almost done. I was tired. I needed a bath. I wanted a gin or six, but we were not done yet. When we left the ship this morning, there had been only one purpose in mind – find Sam.

We were yet to achieve that.

"So where is he?" asked Schneider, the tall Austrian who always treated Sam like a little brother.

"And why don't you look worried anymore?" Barbie wanted to know, the suspicion that I was holding back vital information once again evident on her pretty face.

We were back at the ship where passengers were returning from their exciting day spent ashore. They would have explored the coastline, taken trips – possibly to Haden Falls – and would have been able to sample the local culinary delights. I had done none of that, but could claim that the British Union Isles were a place I would remember forever.

I hadn't answered Barbie's question and she was going to stamp her foot, the good one I presumed, if I didn't spill the beans soon.

Spotting some benches set out by the crew for some of the more elderly to rest on while they queued to get back on the ship, I crossed to them and sat down.

"It was the ghosts, wasn't it?" asked Tempest.

Pleased at how intuitive he always proved to be, I nodded. "Yes."

"What about them?" asked Martin. "I don't get it. Where is Sam?"

Answering him, I posed a question. "Do you think the 'ghost' that stabbed you was trying to kill you?"

Martin shook his head. "No. I guess, on reflection, I don't. He could have killed me easily if he'd wanted to."

"We … I" I corrected myself, "thought they were the police."

"They were the police," argued Deepa, thinking she knew better. "We ran into them again outside that Strawberry Moons place. You are the one who said you saw the cop who got you from your cell last night."

"Different ghosts," I replied. My comment threw everyone, (except Tempest, I was sure) so I explained. "I believe the police chose to dress as the ghosts because we told them all about the attack at the house. It was the perfect cover, and we have all heard how ensconced into local legend the ghosts are. They could kill us, and no one would question it. It was the police today, but not last night." My friends were still struggling to follow my logic. "Everyone has been looking for Edward, which meant that none of the people we were running from had him. The ghosts in his house last night couldn't have been the police because …" I left the sentence hanging to see who would fill in the blank.

Martin got there first. "Because the police turned up minutes later and they were looking for him."

"Exactly," I congratulated him with a wink.

Barbie squealed at me, "Patty! If the ghosts last night weren't the police, then who were they?"

"Some of the other people caught up in the offshore airport scam is my guess." My reply caused my friends to all look at each other in wonder and bewilderment. "We saw a list of names on the wall in his office. I think Edward contacted the other victims and together they hatched a plan. They played the part of the ghosts – the whole thing was staged to get us involved and they knew enough about me or us to grab Sam."

Martin's face folded inward on itself as if he were trying to do some particularly difficult mental math. "Hold on. The police said they were responding to a call from Edward. He told them he was being attacked in his home. That's why Quimby arrested us all in the first place."

"Yes," agreed Deepa, "If he faked the abduction and was taken by his own people, why did he call the police for help, especially since he told us he believed they were dirty …"

"And he was right," cut in Barbie."

"And he was right," agreed Deepa. "And why hasn't he surfaced? And where is Sam?"

My friends were getting frustrated with me, and I couldn't blame them. Normally, when we do this there is a lot of gin and tonic going around to make them all feel more relaxed and less inclined to press me to get to the point.

Jermaine, in tune with me as always, was astute enough to have been observing me. He had seen where I was looking and still standing had a better view than I. It was no surprise when he saw them first.

"Here they are now, madam," he announced.

Everyone swung around to look. Coming through the gate to the docks was Edward and by his side was my assistant. His goofy grin was just where it always ought to be, and the sight of Sam filled my heart.

Barbie spun her wheelchair to block me.

"Right, Patty, that's it! Tell me what happened here and make it fast."

Sam hadn't spotted us yet, the press of people made it harder to pick us out and he probably wasn't looking for us on the quayside. Relenting, I gave them the simple explanation.

"Edward used us. He figured out that if he told me a little about what was happening, and then created his own spooky abduction, I might feel inclined to investigate. He knew DeMeco was coming for him, and he couldn't turn to the police. He took Sam along to ensure there was no way I would choose to not pursue his case and was banking on me figuring the whole thing out. He called the police because he knew full well that we would meet Chief Quimby – I expect Edward was banking on me smelling a rat - and he paid the rickshaw drivers extra to lie about taking us to his house."

Tempest snorted a sorry laugh, "He set things up so you would find yourselves slap bang in the middle of his case."

Alistair shook his head. "That's genius."

I got to my feet. Lifting an arm to wave, I called to get Sam's attention.

He saw me, his own arm shooting skyward to return my wave.

"Mrs Fisher," he called out. "I've been having the best time! Edward took me to a friend's house. They had the latest console and loads of video games, and they let me have ice cream for breakfast!"

Sam came to me, but he wasn't expecting the hug I pulled him into. A tear rolled down my cheek and I held him tightly. When I let him go, I stepped back and took a moment to check him over. He was grinning still – nothing bad had happened to him. No one had been able to find Edward because he was safely tucked away inside the house of a friend. Chief Quimby and Mayor Boxley were unaware of the connection he had with the other victims. Neither did DeMeco for that matter.

Edward was a yard away, waiting respectfully for me to be ready to speak to him.

"Patricia …" he got to say my name.

And I punched him in the face.

Barbie whooped and Jermaine appeared by my side, ready in case Edward thought retaliation was a good idea.

"Owwww!" I cried, looking down at my knuckles. "Oh, my word, that hurts!" I stared at Jermaine. "How do you do that without breaking your hand every time?"

My friends had moved to surround me, giving me comfort with their presence and closeness, but also they were there to give Edward a piece of their collective minds. They had been excited at the prospect of a windfall and ready to sacrifice their time ashore for it. That there had never been any money stung, especially since we had solved the case and saved his neck.

He had lied to us all and put our lives in danger for his own gain. Sam had been safe the whole time, but I couldn't have known that. I had tried to call him many times last night and today, but Edward had confiscated Sam's phone to prevent any of us from contacting him, a tactic that worked perfectly. It kept us in the chase. Edward meant Sam no harm, but would he have got him back to the ship on time if I hadn't solved the case? I would never know the answer and certainly wasn't going to trust what Edward said.

He made apologetic noises but ultimately, we sent him on his way with a flea in his ear. We were weary, but we were back together. I think if we were anywhere else, I would have suggested heading back to my suite. I was still damp from my dip, we were all dirty and dusty from our day, but we had two hours before the ship sailed and that was just long enough to find a restaurant and taste something unique to the island.

We might never get back here again – visits were so rare.

Everyone thought it was a great idea and even Alistair, who was needed back on the ship, chose to come with us. He deferred to his second in command, Commander Ochi, and like Dorothy and pals on the yellow brick road, we all but skipped back out of the port.

I was so caught up in the moment, I never once thought to look around me, but even if I had, would I have noticed that we were being followed?

30

BECOMING DESPERATE

Xavier Silvestre was about as frustrated as he ever got. His plan for the day had not included getting trapped in the morgue for four hours. Having hidden from the nurse when he returned, a doctor then joined him ten minutes later and two paramedics arrived shortly after that when they delivered a patient.

A passenger had tripped, their wrist breaking when they put out an arm to arrest their fall. Had it just been the nurse, Silvestre probably would have killed him and left when he grew impatient, but the patient went into shock and the paramedics, seemingly with nothing better to do, stayed to help in the sickbay.

Five people was too many to ensure he could kill them all swiftly enough that one would not escape and raise an alarm.

When the paramedics finally departed, they took the patient with them, and it wasn't long before the doctor left too. Fingering the hilt of his knife, Silvestre prepared to dispatch the medic, but he got up to leave too, announcing to the old man in the bed that he would be back shortly – he needed a snack from a vending machine.

The old man was still asleep – Silvestre checked to be doubly sure, so his route to escape was clear. However, crossing to the doors, he paused.

How long did he have?

More than a minute for certain.

With swift movements, he went to the computer where he'd seen the doctor and the nurse entering notes. It took but a second to access Finn Murphy's file – all he'd needed to do was enter the man's name in the search bar.

Listening for the nurse to return, Xavier Silvestre had rooted through the drawer under the desk until he found a portable data drive. With the file copied, he'd taken the computer back to the screen it had been on and rushed to get clear of the sickbay.

That was hours ago, and he'd been waiting to catch up with Patricia Fisher ever since. That she continued to elude him so effectively felt almost deliberate. That she might know who he was or what purpose he secretly harboured never entered his mind – he was far too convincing and much too careful for there to be any way for her to know he wasn't the real Professor Noriega.

So her tactic of avoidance was purely coincidental, yet no less frustrating for it.

This morning she had been eating an early breakfast with a room full of people and they looked anxious – pent up energy waiting to be expended. He didn't know what they had been planning, but whatever it was had taken her from the ship while most passengers were still in their beds and had kept her ashore all day.

With additional time to strategize, Silvestre opted to tackle her when she returned to the ship. He had already spent far more time on the stupid, fancy cruise liner than he originally intended, and now they were stuck at one of the few places in the civilised world that did not have an airport. Oh, he could arrange for a seaplane to get him to the Canary Islands and from there it was an easy hop to get back home to Spain, but he couldn't leave until he had what he needed from Patricia Fisher.

All afternoon he waited on the quayside by the ship. Moving around so the security teams managing passengers coming on and off the ship wouldn't become suspicious, he struggled to stay out of sight while also keeping the entrance to the docks in view.

His best chance, he believed, was to get Patricia Fisher before she could get back on board. The mist helped to conceal him while at the same time made it doubly hard to be sure who he was seeing.

However, the hours dragged on, and the mist began to dissipate. When finally his target appeared, his frustration was reaching boiling point and his feet, lower back, and knees were protesting from the hours spent upright.

The surge of relief and excitement lasted only as long as it took to see that she was surrounded by a dozen people. Yet again Patricia Fisher had an entourage with her.

Arguing with himself about how he was going to separate her from them, Silvestre watched when a tall, bald man in his sixties approached her. Her assistant, the one with Downs Syndrome was with him. To Silvestre's great surprise, the small, middle-aged woman from England swung a punch that connected with the bald man's jaw, rocking him back a pace.

Two or three dozen passengers who were passing her all jumped in surprise and there were a few exclamations of shock. Someone from security had witnessed the assault and ran from their post by the ship to intervene.

A man stepped out from the crowd of people around Patricia, waving the security guard away. Silvestre recognised him as the captain. An exchange of words took place, but when Silvestre thought Patricia and her entourage were going to head for the ship, they turned around and went the other way – out through the gates to the quayside.

They were heading back into town.

Buoyed by hope, Silvestre followed.

31

BANQUET

Alistair was the only one of our group who had ever visited the island before, but unlike everywhere else we had ever gone, he wasn't filled with knowledge about wonderful local eateries just around the corner and tucked down a side street.

"Mrs Fisher!"

The joyful exclamation came from beneath the front awning of a shop to our left, and I turned my head to find Freddie with his arms out wide in welcome.

"Mrs Fisher, your costume appears to have suffered some damage. Perhaps I can offer you a new one. Special discount just for you."

Incredibly, I had forgotten that we left our clothes in his shop this morning and would have wearily returned to the ship without reclaiming them had he not called my name.

We all adjusted our trajectory to approach his store. "Freddie, thank you, but I think I will just take my own clothes back. Perhaps you know of somewhere we can find local delicacies to eat? We are all quite hungry."

He met my enquiry with his usual gusto. "But, of course. My cousin's place is just around the corner. I will call him now and reserve a table," he stood on tiptoes to perform a headcount, his lips moving as he moved an index finger through the air, "tables," he concluded. "I will take you there myself. My cousin will give you a generous discount if I introduce you as my friends."

His exuberance made me smile. He had all the energy I lacked.

We reclaimed our clothes and took turns getting changed in the small room he had at the back of the store just as we had this morning. Not that we all needed to switch our outfits. It was only me, Molly and Jermaine who were still dressed as pirates, everyone else had either been in their usual clothes or, like Alistair, were back in uniform for the showdown at the boatshed.

True to his word, Freddie led us to a restaurant just around the corner. It was the sort of place you would walk by a hundred times and never go in, but the food was excellent and the service second to none.

With the time before we were due back on board dwindling, I downed my third gin and tonic and slumped back in my chair. My belly was full, and mine wasn't the only one. Fresh seabass served over local steamed vegetables and a lightly spiced rice dish the locals called 'Hotch' was just the first course in what turned out to be a banquet.

We needed to go, but before we left the restaurant, I also needed to *go*. Excusing myself for a trip to the powder room, I pushed back my chair and levered my aching body back to upright.

"May I be of assistance, madam?" enquired Jermaine, moving to get up.

I waved for him to sit. "This is a one-woman task."

Barbie grunted as she hopped onto her one good foot and got ready to hobble after me.

"Nevertheless," she said, "I'm coming with you."

32

KNIFEPOINT

Little emotion passed through Silvestre's mind during the hour he watched Patricia and her group eat their dinner. The restaurant was nothing more than a shack with a roof woven from palm tree leaves and that played right into his hands. So too did the number of drinks the group was imbibing.

He counted Patricia Fisher downing three large glasses of gin and tonic and knew all he had to do was bide his time and wait for nature to take its course.

Watching from a stool at an open bar across the street, he was ready when Patricia Fisher finally left her chair to head for the ladies' restroom. His bill was paid – not that he touched the rum and coke he ordered just to look the part – so as she vanished through the restroom door, Xavier Silvestre followed.

Her friend, the blonde one with the stunning body and looks, was with her, but she was clearly injured and unlikely to put up much of a fight. He would kill them both if he needed.

At the thought of what would be necessary, he lifted his left hand to touch the ceramic blade – selected because it would not show up on the ship's metal detectors. It was still where he kept it, inside a Velcro pouch inside his right sleeve.

No one noticed him when he slipped into the restaurant through one of the open walls. The place was at least half filled with people enjoying food, and he was just another tourist on his way to the restrooms. That he chose the restroom on the right and not the left went unseen.

Hoping he'd timed it fortuitously so that Patricia Fisher would be washing her hands and have her back to him when he approached, he was disappointed to find the blonde friend instead. He saw why instantly – the low-budget restaurant's facilities included only one cubicle.

A glance showed him the soles of Patricia's Fisher's shoes beneath the stall door. In the half second of indecision, the blonde woman looked up, spotted a man, and smiled at him in the mirror. She was about to say something like 'Wrong room', but Patricia Fisher chose that moment to flush the toilet and Silvestre seized his chance.

He snatched the knife from its pouch and kicked out at the blonde's injured leg.

She squealed in pain and grabbed the sink to support herself.

With his foot, Silvestre kicked the door to the restroom shut and locked it, sealing the three of them inside. He doubted anyone had heard the blonde's cry of pain, but it was a public restroom, and he wanted a few moments of peace to extract what he needed from the English sleuth.

Patricia burst from the cubicle. "Barbie! Are you okay?" She rushed to her friend's side before she spotted the man inside the ladies' restroom with them. "Professor Noriega?" she questioned. "What's going on?"

"Yeah?" seethed Barbie through gritted teeth. "What's going on?"

Silvestre brandished the knife. "I had questions for you this morning, Mrs Fisher. You were too busy to answer them then. Perhaps I will find you more accommodating now." He watched the fear spread on the women's faces. "I want to know where the jewels are, Mrs Fisher. I want to know where they are, what else you found, and everything you know about Finn Murphy and what happened to him."

A polite knocking was followed by Hideki calling through the door. "Babes? Everything all right in there? Did you fall?"

Silvestre cursed silently and took a step toward the two women, the knife menacing the air. "Make him go away." Moving close enough that the blade was inches from their necks, he made it clear how swiftly he could strike if he did not like what the blonde had to say.

Barbie grunted in pain as she shifted her weight, but said, "Yes, *Richard*. I'm fine. I'll be out in a minute. Just go back to your seat and wait for me."

Silvestre had expected one or both to cry for help. He would have killed them, and then the first person to come through the door, but fear had made them hope he might spare their lives if they complied.

Outside, the man there said, "Okay," in a semi-satisfied way and his footsteps could be heard retreating.

Silvestre raised the knife again, touching it to the blonde's neck. "Barbie, is it?" He heard the man outside address her by name. Looking at Patricia, he growled, "Everything you know, or you get to watch your friend die."

Patricia Fisher raised her hands in supplication. "Please," she begged. "There's no need to hurt anyone. I will tell you all that I know."

Silvestre rasped, "No need? There is every need. I have dedicated my life to finding the truth. You cannot begin to fathom what you have stumbled upon. If you test me, I will show you how irrevolent your friend's life is. Now talk!" He pressed the blade a little harder into the blonde's neck.

The only warning they got were some gasps from outside in the restaurant. Patricia knew it was coming, Barbie used a different name when she addressed Hideki – clue enough that they were in trouble. When the wall adjacent to the door exploded inward and three bodies smashed through it, she was ready to yank Barbie away from the knife.

Silvestre reacted the moment he sensed what was happening. He heard the same gasps, and then the faint vibration of feet running on the floor nearby. When the wall burst open, arms and legs flailing at the thin material the building was made from, he launched himself upward onto the sink and then out through the window.

He heard shouting behind him, but never looked back. Within a few seconds, he was a street over and a hundred yards away. He had ditched Professor Noriega's jacket and was wearing a pirate hat and festival beads he'd snatched from a shop's display stand.

Cursing his luck, he knew he had missed his chance. Following his attack, they would head directly back to the ship – it was due to sail soon, after all. He couldn't follow – the chance they would identify him even with a change of outfit was far too high.

He was stuck on the island. He'd learned almost nothing, and there was nothing he could do about it.

The San José was out there, and no one was closer than he. The autopsy report for Finn Murphy provided a new start point. He would contact his assistant, Gomez, get home and from there begin again. Patricia was wilier than he had anticipated, but like her friend, she was irrevolent.

Disappointed with the result, but certain there was nothing more he could have done, Xavier Silvestre took out his phone. It was time to …

A smile spread across his face. If Patricia Fisher was anything, she was a nosey sleuth. She knew him as Professor Noriega of the Museum of Brazil in Rio. The ship was heading there next, and he was willing to bet a fortune that she would be trying to find out why he attacked her.

She would discover the professor had been killed recently and the lure of mystery – knowing the man she met was not the real Professor Noriega, would force her to investigate. He could travel to Rio and be waiting for her.

Pressing the phone to his ear, Xavier Silvestre felt like joining in with the fools dancing in the street.

EPILOGUE

The ship's mighty engines were already running when we got back to the dock. We were rushing to get to the ship in the aftermath of Professor Noriega's attack and in the confusion had forgotten something vital.

"This is where we say goodbye," said Tempest. He and Big Ben had run alongside us as we raced to the docks, but reaching the gates and the additional security represented by the Aurelia's crew beyond, they were stopping.

The crew were urging us to get on board, but I had to impart my gratitude to the two men from England first.

It came as no surprise that when I stopped, so did everyone else – they all wanted to shake the hands of the men who came to help us.

"How can I ever repay you?" I asked, wrapping my arms around Tempest to pull him into a hug.

He chuckled. "There's nothing to repay. It was my pleasure to be of assistance."

"You must send me a bill for your services. It must have cost a bomb to get here at such short notice."

He laughed again. "I shall do no such thing. Consider it a

professional courtesy. Perhaps one day I will have cause to call on you for help."

Next to us Big Ben was shaking hands with Jermaine, Schneider, and the others, but I could see he was looking at Barbie.

Hideki stood behind her wheelchair; his stance relaxed but protective. When the people between Barbie and Big Ben parted, she waved him forward to come and hug her.

"You came all this way just because I sent you a single text asking for your help," she remarked when he came down to her height. "How does a girl repay a kindness like that?"

I tensed, expecting a typical Big Ben line to spill from his mouth. He was an absolute sex pest and she had chosen to feed him an easy opening line. I wasn't the only one now worried for what he might say in front of Hideki – I could see Tempest wincing with anticipation.

Big Ben looked down at the ground, and then back up, reaching out to take Barbie's right hand in both of his.

"I believe, Barbie," he started, his voice soft and tender for once. "That I may search forever and never find a woman I am more besotted with than you."

I almost choked on my surprise, and Barbie's face showed the unexpected emotion she felt.

Big Ben continued. "I'm just sorry I didn't find you sooner." With that, he kissed the knuckles of the hand he held, stood up and offered his hand for Hideki to shake. "Treat her well," he remarked.

Alistair cut in, "Sorry to break this up, everyone, but we really must get on board."

A final hurried exchange of goodbyes and good lucks had to find their way across the divide as we left the Blue Moon boys outside the dock.

Turning around to face the ship I heard Tempest remark, "Ben that is the most honest thing I have ever heard you say."

Big Ben exhaled, a hard breath leaving his body before he clapped his hands together and said, "Right, let's find a bar. There's an entire female population on this island that needs some Big Ben action."

Even though I was hustling to get to the ship, I couldn't help but smile at how quickly he'd reverted back to his usual self.

No sooner did we cross the gangplank than the door began to shut behind us. The ship had to be seaworthy, and a hundred checks conducted before it would slip the dock.

That I had been attacked by Professor Noriega was not in question. What nobody knew was why? Sure he wanted to know about the jewels we found in Finn Murphy's body. Their existence had become public knowledge when Angelica had someone hack my computer and then publish my notes.

That didn't explain coming at me with a knife.

Barbie was shaken but unharmed. There was a small cut beneath her chin, but her ankle hurt worse she assured us.

Finding out who Professor Noriega was and everything that might have driven him to attack us was high on my list of things to do, but it was going to have to wait. He wasn't on the ship – I was fairly certain of that, but he worked at the Museum of Brazil in Rio, and we were heading there right now.

There had been something about him that hadn't sat right from the very first moment we met. I didn't know what it was then, and nothing had changed. He was an enigma I needed to unravel. I could barely remember what he had said, which is unusual for me.

I needed some sleep so I could make my brain work better than it was. Maybe in the morning I would remember more. One thing had stuck though. A single word: irrevolent. He said it wrong. Did that mean anything?

Stepping off the elevator, I turned around and stuck a foot out to hold the doors open.

"You can all go. Please," I begged them. "I'm fine with Jermaine from here. Sam, you need to go find your gran. I texted her earlier, so she knows you are on your way. The rest of you … who knows what tomorrow will bring. Thank you all for being at my side today, but get some rest, please."

They didn't put up much of a fight. If they were half as tired as I felt, they needed to get a shower and go to bed.

The elevator doors swung shut and my friends departed,

returning to their own cabins as I went to mine. Walking the final yards to my suite it occurred to me that not only did I have whatever tomorrow chose to throw at me and the new Professor Noriega mystery to unravel, there was still the Angelica dilemma to manage. My tactic of leaving the ship had worked beautifully – she hadn't been able to do anything to me or to any of my friends because we were out of reach.

However, the moment Jermaine buzzed my door open, I knew there was something amiss.

"Girls?" I called into the darkness.

Jermaine stepped around me, striding into the suite and flicking on lights.

"Anna? Georgie?" Cold fear spread outward from my heart, filling my veins with ice as I moved into the suite myself.

Seeing a pair of shoe-clad feet poking out from behind a couch, I gasped, my hand flying to my mouth.

Jermaine got there a heartbeat later, checking the body though it was hidden from sight by the couch itself.

"He's alive," Jermaine announced, pulling out his phone to call for help. I ran to his side.

Lieutenant Kashmir had a lump on his head the size of a tennis ball. The skin had split, but was not open. It had bled, but the discharge was mostly plasma. He was coming around now that Jermaine was touching him.

I ran to my bedroom, calling for the girls to answer me and checked all the rooms including Jermaine's adjoining butler's cabin before accepting that my dogs were gone.

"What happened?" I begged to know when I got back to the living area to find Kashmir now sitting on the couch rather than lying behind it.

Jermaine handed him a towel filled with ice which he held to the lump on his head. Kashmir's eyes were closed, the light in the room probably hurting his brain, but he managed to explain, "A cleaner came. I didn't know her, but there are always new crewmembers. I figured she was one of those who joined the ship in Lanzarote. The moment my back was turned, she hit me with something. I don't remember anything else." He sighed, a sorrowful exhalation of air. "She took the dogs, didn't she?"

A knock at the door preceded the arrival of two paramedics. I stepped out of their way to let them work and it was then that I spotted the note on my desk.

'*The Patricia Fisher show is over. I have your dogs and you are going to dance to my tune now. Stand by for instructions. Angelica.*'

I closed my eyes and wept.

The End

AUTHOR'S NOTES

Dear Reader,

Thank you once again for reading all the way to the end. Writing this book has genuinely felt like something of a mission. Not that it is a long book, though it ranks in the top twenty percent of Patricia adventures by length, but because of how many sleepless nights it has taken to finish.

I had a good go at closing it out yesterday. That was a Monday. I had wanted it finished last week, but the hours to get it done eluded me, so yesterday I committed to carrying on until it was done.

At one o'clock this morning with more than eleven thousand new words added, I had to admit I was beaten. My brain was getting foggy, and I worried the words might not make sense. It was a good thing I did stop because it took a further four hours of writing this morning to reach the end.

Stories are like that – you just never know how long they will need to be to get the tale told.

I hope you enjoyed it. It was a blast for me to include Tempest and Big Ben, two of my very first character creations and ones which will always have a special place in my heart. Getting the balance right so each character's individual skills and nuances come across is a tough thing to achieve when you have so many different ones in a single book. Adding Tempest and Big Ben made that harder, but I am pleased with the result.

Edward Teach really was Blackbeard the pirate. If you are ever near Beaufort in North Carolina, they have a wonderful museum there with a section dedicated to him. Or they did when I was last there in 2004.

Finding someone on a ship. I was once in Norfolk, Virginia where the USS Wisconsin sits as a floating museum. While many of my army colleagues there with me that day chose to frequent watering hole after watering hole, I broadened my horizons and was regaled with a tale of two men who joined the US Navy together. Stationed aboard the same ship, the newly commissioned USS Wisconsin, an Iowa Class battleship, one proceeded to try to find the other.

This was during the final months of the Second World War. After days of fruitless searching, that crewman chose to write a letter instead, the missive finally achieving what feet and eyeballs could not. Like so many things that enter my head, that tale got stuck, and became the basis for Patricia's inability to locate Angelica.

In this book I write a scene where Tempest Michaels is reading the ground via topography. If this sounds far-fetched, I can assure you it is not. In fact, it is a skill I myself learned in the army, once winning an orienteering competition without a compass to guide me.

I also mention cockney rhyming slang but cannot for the life of me recall if I have ever explained it before. My apologies if I am now repeating myself. Basically, in place of a word like 'believe', a cockney (the name given to a person born within earshot of Bow Bell in London) would say Adam and Eve.

Would you Adam and Eve it? Cash becomes 'Pie and Mash'. Pocket becomes 'Skyrocket'. The why of it is completely lost on me, but writing Gloria, her use of 'Cream Crackered' in lieu of knackered seemed entirely in keeping with her character.

As I finish up this book, the temperature outside is climbing. The start of spring is days away, but the garden couldn't be bothered to wait for the calendar. Hunter and I cleaned out the greenhouse last weekend and planted a bunch of seeds and some seedlings we got from the local garden centre, plus herbs, potatoes, and goodness knows what else.

At six, my son believes he is an old hand at growing a harvest of vegetables, but then he can claim to have been doing it for more than half his life. My almost two-year-old daughter, Hermione, joined in for the first time, helpfully stomping around in my freshly dug vegetable beds.

I still find it remarkable that my son is the biggest kid in his class by a large margin, loves dinosaurs, noise, and karate, but is the gentlest giant you could ever meet, yet my petite, pink princess can be found downloading bombmaking instructions from the internet.

I fear for her teen years.

Take care.

Steve Higgs

WHAT'S NEXT FOR PATRICIA

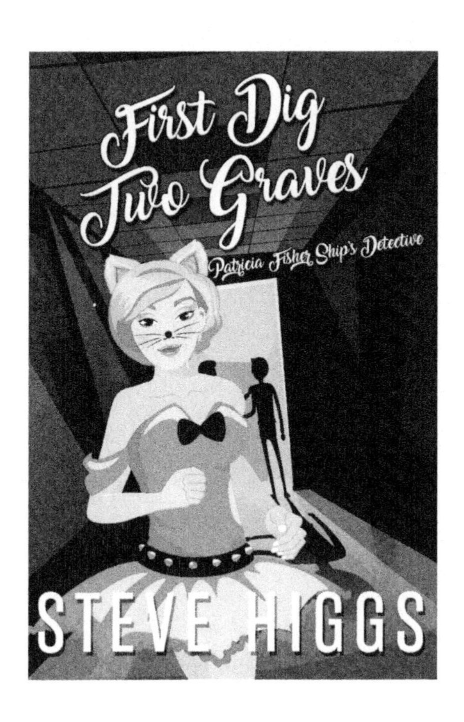

If you devote your life to seeking revenge …

Whether Confucius had it right or not is of little consequence to

Patricia Fisher right now because she's on the run from multiple criminals plus the cruise ship's security team who have orders to arrest her on sight.

Her arch nemesis, Angelica Howard-Box, has finally figured out how to win and she is going all out to make Patricia's life a living hell.

Dressed in a pink anime kitten outfit, cut off from her friends, and forced to perform ridiculous tasks because Angelica is suddenly holding all the cards. It's Patricia's toughest challenge yet, and she must race against time if she wants to find a way to turn the tables.

MORE COZY MYSTERY

Marriage? It can be absolute murder.

Wedding planner for the rich and famous, Felicity Philips is aiming to land the biggest gig of her life – the next royal wedding. But there are a few obstacles in her way …

… not least of which is a dead body the police believe she is responsible for murdering.

Out of custody, but under suspicion, her rivals are lining up to ruin her name. With so much on the line, she needs to prove it wasn't her and fast. But that means finding out who the real killer is …

… without said killer finding out what she is up to.

With Buster the bulldog as her protector and Amber the ragdoll cat providing sartorial wit – mostly aimed at the dog - Felicity is turning sleuth.

What does a wedding planner know about solving a crime?

Nothing. Absolutely nothing.

BLUE MOON INVESTIGATIONS

The paranormal? It's all nonsense but proving it might just get them all killed.

When a master vampire starts killing people in his hometown, paranormal investigator, Tempest Michaels, takes it personally …

… and soon a race against time turns into a battle for his life.

He doesn't believe in the paranormal but has a steady stream of clients with cases too weird for the police to bother with. Mostly it's all nonsense, but when a third victim turns up with bite marks in her lifeless throat, can he really dismiss the possibility that this time the monster is real?

Joined by an ex-army buddy, a disillusioned cop, his friends from the pub, his dogs, and his mother (why are there no grandchildren, Tempest), our paranormal investigator is going to stop the murders if it kills him …

… but when his probing draws the creature's attention, his family and friends become the hunted.

MORE BOOKS BY STEVE HIGGS

Blue Moon Investigations

Paranormal Nonsense
The Phantom of Barker Mill
Amanda Harper Paranormal Detective
The Klowns of Kent
Dead Pirates of Cawsand
In the Doodoo with Voodoo
The Witches of East Malling
Crop Circles, Cows and Crazy Aliens
Whispers in the Rigging
Bloodlust Blonde – a short story
Paws of the Yeti
Under a Blue Moon – A Paranormal Detective Origin Story
Night Work
Lord Hale's Monster
The Herne Bay Howlers
Undead Incorporated
The Ghoul of Christmas Past
The Sandman
Jailhouse Golem

Shadow in the Mine
Ghost Writer

Patricia Fisher Cruise Mysteries

The Missing Sapphire of Zangrabar
The Kidnapped Bride
The Director's Cut
The Couple in Cabin 2124
Doctor Death
Murder on the Dancefloor
Mission for the Maharaja
A Sleuth and her Dachshund in Athens
The Maltese Parrot
No Place Like Home
What Sam Knew
Solstice Goat
Recipe for Murder
A Banshee and a Bookshop
Diamonds, Dinner Jackets, and Death
Frozen Vengeance
Mug Shot
The Godmother
Murder is an Artform
Wonderful Weddings and Deadly Divorces
Dangerous Creatures
Patricia Fisher: Ship's Detective
Fitness Can Kill
Death by Pirates

Albert Smith Culinary Capers

Pork Pie Pandemonium
Bakewell Tart Bludgeoning
Stilton Slaughter
Bedfordshire Clanger Calamity
Death of a Yorkshire Pudding
Cumberland Sausage Shocker

Arbroath Smokie Slaying
Dundee Cake Dispatch
Lancashire Hotpot Peril
Blackpool Rock Bloodshed
Kent Coast Oyster Obliteration
Eton Mess Massacre

Felicity Philips Investigates

To Love and to Perish
Tying the Noose
Aisle Kill Him
A Dress to Die for
Wedding Ceremony Woes

Real of False Gods

Untethered magic
Unleashed Magic
Early Shift
Damaged but Powerful
Demon Bound
Familiar Territory
The Armour of God
Terrible Secrets
Top Dog
Hellfire Hellion

Printed in Great Britain
by Amazon